"Jesus! Did burnt?" Heart pounding, he leaped forward, landing on his knees. Without thought to impropriety, he lifted her dress to check her legs for burns.

"Should I get the balm?" Flipping the material over his shoulder, his hands moved over the white, smooth skin, searching for red blisters or welts.

The back door flew open, hitting the wall with a smack. "Hey boss, we gotta talk about this new fella you brought home."

Kid turned to the sound, one hand fought to push frayed material out of his eyes. Flour dust puffed from the fabric as he batted it aside. When it settled, draping his head and shoulders, he stared up at Joe.

"Oh, uh, sorry!" Joe turned beet red and shot back out the door.

Blood rushed to his cheeks, burning and tingling. Had he just been caught with his head under her skirt? Something under his fingers trembled, making him realize one hand was still wrapped around her leg. All of a sudden his fingers felt like they were on fire.

Blowing out a gust of air, Kid pulled his fingers from her shin and backed out from beneath her skirt. "You, um." He paused, cleared his throat. "You didn't get burnt?" It hadn't helped, he sounded like a croaking frog.

"No, no, I didn't."

Frozen- like a petrified rock- he stayed there, on his hands and knees, staring at the varnished wood floor. After the universe had tick-tocked what felt like an hour, but most likely was less than a minute, he stood and taking the chance his weather-beaten face wouldn't show his embarrassment, looked at her.

"What happened?"

Reviews for Lauri Robinson's other stories...

"...a gripping story about true love..."
~The Romance Studio review of A Wife for Big John.

"Lauri Robinson has turned the tables on mail order forever."
~Two Lips Reviews on Mail Order Husband.

"Ms. Robinson has written a delightful and witty tale with an eastern-born hero any cowgirl is going to love. I look forward to more from Lauri Robinson."
~Carol Aloisi, LoveWesternRomances.com on Mail Order Husband

Shotgun Bride

by

Lauri Robinson

This is a work of fiction. Names, characters, places, and incidents are either the product of the author's imagination or are used fictitiously, and any resemblance to actual persons living or dead, business establishments, events, or locales, is entirely coincidental.

Shotgun Bride

COPYRIGHT © 2008 by Lauri Robinson

All rights reserved. No part of this book may be used or reproduced in any manner whatsoever without written permission of the author or The Wild Rose Press except in the case of brief quotations embodied in critical articles or reviews.

Contact Information: info@thewildrosepress.com

Cover Art by *Nicola Martinez*

The Wild Rose Press
PO Box 708
Adams Basin, NY 14410-0706
Visit us at www.thewildrosepress.com

Publishing History
First Cactus Rose Edition, 2008
Print ISBN 1-60154-368-9

Published in the United States of America

Dedication

To my half dozen brothers,
I know none of you would have traded me
for a horse...Right?
Love to all,
Lauri

Southwestern Kansas
1880

Chapter One

Jessie Johnson stared down the barrel of a shotgun. Her mouth felt stuffed with cotton, so dry there was nothing to swallow. Light from the oil lamp on the table glistened off the metal of the double barrels. She tried to swallow again. Her tongue stuck to the roof of her mouth.

The lopsided door creaked, coming to rest against the wall. The night sky, as black as coal, filled the doorway while her arms rose to fold over her chest in meager protection. She squinted into the darkness.

Vaguely, a sinister silhouette, holding the stock firm and steady, took shape. Trembles pulled on her bottom jaw. A thousand thoughts jumbled together. Not a one formed into words.

"You Jessie Johnson?" a raspy voice broke the heavy silence.

Nodding, she unstuck her tongue and answered, "Y-yes." Why hadn't she peeked out the side window before opening the thick door of the sod shanty? She knew better. But in the three months they'd lived on the Kansas prairie, there hadn't been a single visitor. Caution had slipped away with the ever-flowing wind.

"Good, you're the one I want," the voice said.

Jessie frowned. "Excuse me?"

The gun came forward. The chill of cold metal penetrated the material of her dress as the tip of the barrel touched her left shoulder. A tingle zipped up her back.

The harsh voice said, "You're the one I came for. Let's go!"

Jessie snuck two fingers over, slipping them between cold metal and worn cotton and said, "I'm sorry, I can't go anywhere with you. I'm the only one here. My brother will be home soon. He-"

"Ya need some help there, Ma?" a deep voice, definitely male, asked from somewhere in the darkness.

"Hold your horses, Skeeter! Give me a minute here," the gun holder shouted before giving the barrel another nudge, which pinned Jessie's shaky fingers against her collarbone. "I know your brother ain't here. He's at my place."

The pulse in her neck increased. "He is?" Both temples pounded. "R-Russell's at your place?" A thick, solid lump formed in her throat. "W-Who are you?"

"I'm Stephanie Quinter. And yeah, Russell's over at our place. And that's where you're going too."

"Why? Is he hurt?" she asked, a flicker of hope tickling her chest.

Stephanie Quinter jabbed the gun forward again. "Not yet, but he's gonna be if'n you don't get over to my place right quick."

The flicker of hope snuffed out. Wishing she could run, but with nowhere to go in the one room shanty, she stepped backwards. "Why? What has he done?" A deep, sinking feeling hit the pit of her stomach like a rock. She'd checked with the land office, and knew they weren't squatting on the Quinter's land. But that was of little consequence, when it came to Russell, there's very little that would surprise her. She took another step backwards.

The woman and the gun followed, stepping into

the light from the tiny flame of the lantern on the table. Between a brimmed bonnet, tied with a large bow beneath a double chin and the wide, wooden stock of the gun tucked tightly against a dark, knitted shawl, most of Stephanie Quinter's face remained hidden. Pointed leather toes curled up at an odd angle below the hem of a paisley print dress. Short, round, and past middle age, the woman clomped forward on men's work boots.

Sick to her stomach, Jessie sighed. "Mrs. Quinter," she began while moving closer to the rickety table. "I'm sorry for whatever my brother may have done, but I assure you, I had nothing to do with it."

Stephanie Quinter lifted her chin. Huge, grey-green eyes looked Jessie up and down before they narrowed and dark brows furrowed. "You know how to read?"

Somewhat confused by the change of subject, Jessie nodded.

"And write?"

"Yes, Ma'am."

"What about numbers? You know 'bout them?"

"Yes," Jessie answered. Stephanie Quinter wasn't nearly as frightening in the full light of the lamp. Her eyes looked tired and her face haggard. A stab of regret for whatever Russell may have done to the older woman pierced Jessie's chest. *Dang him!* She really wanted to stay here. The constant running of the past few years had long ago grown tiresome.

"Good, I think you'll do right nicely for my Kid." Stephanie Quinter waved the barrel of the gun. "Let's go."

"Your kid?" Jessie grabbed the back of the only chair in the room. If Russell had hired her out as a school marm again, she'd kill him. There was too much to do before winter set in. The little sod house needed so much work. She refused to go into the long, cold months without adequate food this year.

"Yeah, at first I's thinkin' it'd be Skeeter, but now I'm thinkin' it'll be Kid." Stephanie Quinter nodded toward the table. "Blow out the light. We gotta go. There's gonna be a storm 'afore long."

"Mrs. Quinter, I wish I could help you, but I can't. I have too much to do here. Perhaps next spring we could work something out, but right now, it's just not possible."

Quicker than a snake striking, the woman's hand reached out and grabbed. Firm fingers wrapped around her upper arm and tugged. "You ain't too bright is ya?"

Jessie stumbled forward then caught her footing and dug worn heels into the dirt floor to make the woman stop. "Excuse me?"

"What's takin' so long?" A tall, gangly man stepped through the open door. Unruly hair stuck out in all directions under the rim of a floppy hat.

Stephanie shot the man a nasty look. "I told ya to hold your horses!"

"There's a storm brewing, lightning's bouncing all over out there. What's takin' so long, anyhow?" He leaned one arm against the doorframe. The thinness of his face made each line look sharp and pointed. Deep-set eyes started at Jessie's toes and a wide, wicked smile formed on narrow lips as the stony gaze ended on her face. "Is this the sister?"

"Ya, but I changed my mind, she ain't for you. She's for Kid," the woman said.

"Aw, Ma, come on." The smile on his face turned upside down and tattered boots scuffled as he whined, "Kid don't need her none."

"Um, Mrs. Quinter-" Jessie started.

"We've jawed enough." Stephanie Quinter's hand turned to steel. "Here, take her to the horses."

Thrust forward, her heels couldn't catch ground

before rough hands grabbed both shoulders. Jessie twisted, but his grasp was as strong as his mother's. A snide laugh bolted from his lips as his fingers dug into her flesh. A shiver rose up her spine as Stephanie Quinter blew out the lamp and darkness shrouded the tiny sod house. The man pushed and she stumbled over the threshold. The thud of the thick door echoed into the night as he forced her to walk across uneven ground. Blinking didn't help, the blackness surrounding them made everything invisible.

A flash of lightning, far off on the horizon, did little to lighten the area. She bowed her head, it really didn't matter, light or dark, she didn't have much hope. Russell had struck again. Her toe stubbed a rock, and the hands squeezed harder.

Twisting against the brutality, Jessie lifted her chin. "Mrs. Quinter, please, there must be some misunderstanding. Perhaps we could go back in the house. I'll make us some tea." Fully aware of the fact she didn't have any tea, but did have a few white sage leaves she could boil, she continued, "I'm sure we can settle whatever problem my brother may have caused if we just sit down and talk about it."

Stephanie Quinter let out a rough guffaw. "See, Skeeter, she's too bright for you. She's just like Kid, always tryin' to talk things through." Two horses a few feet in front of them came into view as the woman spoke again, "Here, tie her hands behind her back and put her on my horse."

Rough hands slid down her sleeves then pulled her wrists behind her back, straining her shoulders in their sockets. Jessie twisted at the pain. The man named Skeeter tugged harder and began to wrap something around her wrists. A tight knot made her shoulder blades form a v in her back and caused the material of her dress to stretch across her breasts. She wiggled and tucked her chin to her chest, fearful the buttons holding the worn material together might pop.

"She can ride with me," Skeeter said.

Fear deeper than when she'd opened the door to the double barrel shotgun threatened to make her knees buckle.

Skeeter's hat flew off as Stephanie Quinter cuffed the back of his head. "I said put her on my horse and that's what I meant. Now quit stalling. The storm's gettin' closer!"

Without warning, Jessie left the ground. Of their own accord, her legs parted to straddle the leather seat as her bottom landed in a saddle. She folded over the horn, pressing her chest to the leather to keep from slipping off.

A split second later, the saddle tugged sideways. Leaning the opposite way, she bit her lip to keep from suggesting someone tighten the girth strap. Leather creaked as Stephanie Quinter climbed on behind her. The saddle straightened as the woman slid her feet into the stirrups and pushed the shotgun into a long, leather pouch. The front swells of the saddle pressed against Jessie's hip bones as the woman made enough room for both of them in the seat and short arms reached around to take the reins looped over the saddle horn.

Skeeter continued to mumble under his breath, but mounted his horse, and then caught up to ride beside them as they cantered out of the yard. Jessie pressed her knees against the leather, and Stephanie's arms tightened around her, keeping her secure in the saddle as they traveled away from the soddy.

Far away, where the great flat land met an endless sky, flashes of lightning danced like fireflies. The bolts little more than jagged strips of light. The sight wasn't new. Heat lightning often filled the Kansas summer sky. The further they rode, the heavier the night air grew. Jessie let out a long slow breath. The woman was right, a storm brewed. Or had Stephanie Quinter been referring to the squabble with her brother? She tucked her chin to her chest and closed her eyes.

What had Russell done this time? For the past ten years he'd found more trouble than a nosey hound. No, that wasn't quite right. He'd *created* more trouble than a nosey hound. Since she'd been eight years old, his actions had been tearing apart her life.

It had been so long since she knew a normal life. When cholera struck their parents, within three days of each other, she and Russell had been left with a profitable business outside Independence, Missouri. Near where the river turned north and pioneers unloaded wagons from the steamships to prepare for their trip west. Each spring the small city became a boomtown while the wagon trains formed. Jessie remembered those happier times so often, she wondered sometimes if they were dreams instead of memories.

Russell had been fifteen and attempted to take over where their father left off. In less than five years the money, the business, and their home were gone. With little more than the clothes on their backs, they left Independence, begging passage with one of the wagons heading west. Russell said they were moving to a new home and business. At thirteen, Jessie had been too young to know what had all transpired, but a gut feeling said Russell's conniving was the reason they had to leave Independence. It was also why the wagon train deserted them in the middle of Kansas.

For the past five years, they'd traveled from town to town. Sometimes finding abandoned homesteads to live in, but before long one of Russell's deals would back fire, and they'd have to leave again. When Jessie found the soddy eighty miles west of Dodge City- a place where she thought they'd both be killed for sure- she'd told him no more. She wasn't leaving again, no matter how much trouble he found himself in. And she meant it.

Two months ago, she'd walked ten miles into the small town of Nixon and claimed the uninhabited cabin as her own. Kansas wasn't as stringent as other states; they allowed single women to own property. The state had even given women the right to vote in school district elections several years ago.

The clerk at the land office said the land was hers for claiming, as well as the contents of the small shack. When the previous owner had died, his wife left everything to return to her family. Everything wasn't much, but at least they had the basic home furnishings and a roof over their heads- more than what they'd had for a long time.

Jessie had scraped out a small garden and penned in a few prairie chickens, but the most significant thing about the soddy was the fresh water well out back- a precious commodity on the prairie. She had such high hopes of staying put this time.

Something bounced off her cheek, bringing her thoughts to the present and accenting living happily at the soddy wasn't likely to happen. A low rumble of thunder ricocheted across the land and large drops of rain began to fall. The woman behind her heeled the horse into a faster run, and Jessie bent her head again, this time against the weather.

A short time later they arrived at a homestead. The horse skidded to a halt, and Stephanie Quinter pulled Jessie from the horse at the same time she dismounted. Startled by the unexpected, swift movements, she tried to catch her balance, but the slimy ground sent her feet askew. The wet material of her dress clung to her trembling legs, and the tight rope twisted about her wrists made stability impossible. Prepared to hit the ground, Jessie let out a small yelp. The woman grabbed her shoulder to keep her from falling. With more speed than Stephanie Quinter seemed capable of, she was towed through the sheets of rain and into a small house.

The warm glow of a coal oil lamp lit the room. Jessie flipped her head to toss wet strands of hair from her face. Dry and comfortable, Russell lounged in front of a stone fireplace. Mad enough to spit nails, she shook her head, trying to stop water from dripping into her eyes. As the words formed in her mind, they flew from her mouth, "What have you done this time?"

"Sit down," Stephanie gave Jessie a slight push toward the closest chair.

Jessie sat, but her glare never left her brother.

Another man, sitting next to Russell said, "That's your sister, Russ?"

Her brother nodded. "Yes, but I assure you, she's much prettier when she ain't soak 'n wet."

Jessie's lips puckered as she glared harder. She felt like a drowned rat and probably looked like one too. Her waist length hair must be as tangled as a horse's tail after the speedy ride across the flatlands, but her brother didn't have to point it out. Her fingers itched to wrap around his bony neck and squeeze. She turned to the woman hanging a dripping bonnet and cloak on a wooden peg. "Mrs. Quinter, may I be untied now?"

Stephanie Quinter walked over and picked up the shotgun she'd set on the table then turned to hang it on the wall beside the door. "No, I don't think so. Not yet anyway."

"I promise I won't move. The rope is extremely tight." The door beside her flew open. Wind and rain blew in. She crouched at the water slapping against her.

"Damn it, Skeeter! Can't you do anything right? Shut the door, you're gettin' my floor wet," Stephanie Quinter shouted with annoyance.

Jessie looked at the wooden floor, a luxury her soddy didn't have. Overall, the cabin was solidly built, not a drip nor drop of rain found its way in. Long streams of muddy water were most likely flowing down the walls of her sod home. Her gaze continued to make a full circle of the large room. Two doors, one on each end wall, led to what she assumed were bedrooms, and a ladder rose to a loft above. Though small, the home was as neat and clean as the finest mansion.

"Look at that. Her hands are white. You tied the rope so tight it's cuttin' off the blood flow." A loud thump sounded the same time as Stephanie's words. Jessie knew Skeeter had been smacked again even before she heard his whine. Hands began to loosen the rope behind her back.

She took a deep breath. It was as if a thousand red-hot needles had been shoved into her hands. Huffing through the pain, she waited for the ropes to fall from her wrists.

"There, that better?" Stephanie stepped in front of her, reached out and patted one cheek. "Sorry 'bout that, I should have checked the knot sooner."

Jessie wiggled her hands. Trying to rub them together and ease the stinging. Ropes still restrained her wrists, just not as tight. She glanced toward Russell, noticing for the first time his hands were tied behind his back as well.

He grimaced and lifted his shoulders. It was his classic 'Sorry, I screwed up again' look. Jessie let out a deep sigh. She'd been waiting for the other shoe to drop. The past three months had been too quiet, too perfect. She closed her eyes. What has he done this time?

"Your brothers back yet?" Stephanie asked.

"No, Ma, ain't seen 'em yet," the man sitting beside Russell answered. The voice sounded more like a teenager than a man. Jessie peeked through her lashes, but a shadow from the stone wall fell across his face, making it hard to tell.

"Good, you and Skeeter go get Kid." Stephanie began to dip water out of a bucket and pour it into a coffee pot.

"Kid? What we gotta get Kid for? He ain't gonna like this." His head shook from side to side.

Jessie glanced to the loft, wondering how a child could sleep through the ruckus of the house. A tinge of sorrow softened her fear, imagining how the kid they spoke of was probably hiding beneath the covers, frightened to death.

"He'll like it just fine once he finds out we got her for him." Stephanie scooped ground coffee into the pot then set it on the stove.

"For Kid? What does Kid want with her? Does he know about Miss Molly?" The skinny frame rising from the chair was that of a teenager, not quite a kid, not quite a man. Lamp light bounced off dark eyes wide with shock, or was it fear?

"Get off your arse and go get Kid!" Stephanie twisted, grabbed a broom, and whacked the boy with the straw end. He covered the back of his head with both hands as another wallop hit and scrambled toward the door.

"Ma, we can't go get Kid. It's really raining out there," Skeeter said as the boy skidded to a halt behind him.

"Yeah, and it's only gonna get worse. Now go get Kid 'afore the lightning and wind hits."

"But Ma, Kid ain't gonna come with us. You know that." Skeeter reached behind his back and pulled the boy to stand in front of him. Quicker than a fly, the younger boy shot back behind Skeeter, the two of them continued to try and use the other for a shield as their mother stomped across the room.

"Well, if'n you know what's good for ya, you'll figure out a way to get him here. And be quick about it!" She went after both of her sons with the broom.

"I still don't think it's fair. You said I could have her." Skeeter scrambled out the door as the whisk of the broom hit the younger one again.

Stephanie Quinter shouted into the rain, "And what would you do with a woman this fine? You ain't got no idea how she needs to be treated." She turned to Jessie, a smile softening her haggard face. "But Kid does. You'll make him a good wife."

"Wife?" Jessie choked on the word as the door slammed shut.

Chapter Two

Kid Quinter settled the last clean dish into the cupboard and turned to the black dog lying under the table. "That was a right fine meal, Sammy, if I say so myself." The big hound crawled out and walked over to heel by his dust covered boots. Kid grinned as Sammy's head tilted to accept the hand rubbing his ear.

"You tired too, boy? I know I am. It's been a long week, but it was a good drive. Got us some good stock this time, but like you, I'm glad to be home." He gave the dog one final pat. "Come on, time for bed." Before they left the room, Kid blew out the lamp on the table, as well as the one on the wall by the sink. He picked the third one off the counter to light his way though the house and up the stairs to his bedroom.

Five years ago, he'd built the large, solid home. The kind a cattle baron would live in. The house he'd always wanted. It had taken time and a lot of hard work, but he'd done it. And he was well on his way to being a baron. Pride filled his chest at the thought of both accomplishments. A twitch pulled at his cheek. If only his father were here to see it- to see what you could accomplish when you set your mind to it.

Halfway through the front room Sammy left his side. The dog ran to the front door, barking. "You already went out for the night old man, it's time for bed." Kid kept walking toward the stairway.

The pitch of Sammy's bark changed. Kid stilled and turned. "Someone's here?" He looked from the dog to the door. "Who'd be out on a night like this?"

Sammy growled. The hair on the back of Kid's neck tingled as it rose to stand on end. "You've got to be kidding me." Sammy only growled like that when one of his brothers was at the door. The dog didn't care for any of his four younger siblings.

With a heavy sigh, Kid crossed the room, opened the door, and stepped into the night, the wide porch roof protecting him from the pouring rain.

Soaked to the gills, Skeeter and Bug stomped up the front steps. "Hey, Kid. How was Dodge?" Bug took his hat off and shook the water from it.

"Fine, what are you two doing here? There's a serious storm brewing." Kid hung the lantern on the peg outside the door, glancing at a sky filled with long, sharp flashes of lightning. Far off thunder rumbled like an old man snoring.

"Yeah, we heard you was home and just thought we'd be neighborly." Skeeter removed his hat and shook his head. Water flayed from his mop of dirt-blond hair.

"Yeah sure, what's Ma need?" Kid rubbed his forehead. Their overly friendly banter did little more than irritate.

"She needs you to come over to our place…tonight." Bug replaced his wet hat.

Sammy pressed against the back of Kid's knee. A low growl came from his snarled lip. Kid patted the dog's head, but kept his leg between the dog and his brothers. "I'll ride over in the morning. I just got home. I'm too tired to deal with whatever it is tonight."

"Ma said we can't come home without you," Skeeter said.

"Then don't go home. You can sleep here."

"Really?" The hope in Bug's young voice was clearly evident. The youngest of the five brothers, had turned sixteen this past spring. Of all his brothers, Skeeter, Snake, Hog, and Bug, Bug was his favorite. The one he held the most hope in becoming a man, making a go at life.

Skeeter's leg shot out and kicked Bug in the shin. "No, we can't spend the night. Ma needs you now, Kid."

In one swift movement, he stepped forward and grabbed Skeeter's skinny shoulder. Sammy shot out the door. His bared teeth came within inches of Skeeter's leg as another deep growl emitted. Kid ignored the dog and gave Skeeter's arm a hard squeeze. "I've told you before, Bug's not a punching bag for you. Keep your hands and feet off him."

Skeeter backed away from both Kid and Sammy, stopping before he slipped off the porch stairs. "S-sorry, Kid. I-I ain't hit him for a long time." He shook his head and pointed to Bug. "Ask him. Bug, tell Kid I haven't hurt ya lately. Tell him I've been nice." His voice sounded like a screeching fiddle.

"He's telling the truth, Kid. He ain't hurt me none since you told him to quit picking on me," Bug said.

Kid rubbed the back of his neck. Sammy growled again, and Skeeter's shivering increased. He was too tired to put up with his brothers and mother tonight. Whatever she needed would have to wait until morning. It couldn't be too important anyway, nothing ever was.

Stephanie Quinter was a rough, but simple woman. Try as he might, he couldn't refine her. Couldn't make her see there was more to life than living in a shanty and raising a crude crop of grain every year, just as he'd never been able to convince his father of anything different.

Twelve years ago, on his sixteenth birthday, he'd

left home to claim his own lot of land. In reality, Kid hadn't gone far, just a few miles to the plot next to his folks, where he built a soddy. But in his mind, he'd traveled to the other side of the universe and began to study up on owning cattle.

Two years later, when the cattle drives started to roll into Dodge from all directions, he'd been ready to buy the leftovers, the cattle too puny to sell to the stockyards, as well as the pregnant and young ones. Then in the winter, when the prices were high, and the inventory low, he sold them to the yards himself. By then he'd nurtured them into top of the line cattle. The Triple Bar Ranch now had a good base of breeding stock, a fine house, two barns, and several outbuildings. His dream of being a cattle baron was so close to becoming a reality, he could almost claim it.

Low growls pulled his mind back to the porch. Kid slapped his thigh, when Sammy looked his way, he pointed to the open doorway. The dog's tail fell between his back legs and with his head hanging low, he ambled into the house. Sammy's action made a twinge of guilt creep across his chest. He didn't want the dog to think he was in trouble, but he couldn't talk to his brothers with the constant barking and growling. "Good dog," he said as he closed the door behind the lab.

He turned to his brothers in time to catch a glimpse of a flat board swinging through the air. Kid ducked, but it was too late. Pain exploded across the side of the head. "Shit!" he exclaimed the moment before everything went black.

****

The storm had grown. The way the wind and rain beat against the outside of the wooden shelter made Jessie wonder if the shanty would withhold the weather. Lightning regularly lit the windows, simultaneously thunder made the glass pane shake.

The constant booming and rattling made her head hurt even more. Anger and disbelief had triggered the blood pounding in her temples to grow into deep, throbbing pains.

Her protests of becoming anyone's wife had fallen on deaf ears. The other two Quinter brothers, Snake and Hog, had returned earlier, soaking wet, and towing a preacher and sheriff. The hope that grew at seeing the pot-bellied lawman quickly diminished when Stephanie Quinter presented her case, and the sheriff agreed the woman was acting within the law.

Tears hadn't fallen- yet. All the deals her brother had been involved in couldn't compare with this last one. He was literally trading her for a horse. *A horse!* When her wrists were finally untied, she would tear him apart. Shred him from limb to limb. Feed his carcass to the buzzards...

The door flew open and stalled her thoughts. The other brothers had returned. Skeeter and the younger boy, she now knew was named Bug, struggled to carry a large man, who twisted and bucked like a wild animal in their arms, through the open doorway. Jessie ignored the wind and rain as she twisted her tied wrists, feeling lucky only her hands were tied. This man was bound from head to toe. Ropes not only tied his hands behind his back, but they were wrapped around his body from shoulder to ankle, and a wet bandana covered his mouth. The material puffed as indistinct mumbles came from the man.

Stephanie hit Hog, or maybe it was Snake, on the back of the head. "Get up and help your brothers." Her hand caught the other brother on the back swing. "You get the door."

Their chairs uprooted as they jumped to do as instructed. It took all four of them to get the bound and gagged man into a chair at the table next to her.

One produced another rope and wound it around the man's legs and chest, securing him to the chair. The wooden legs bounced and skidded across the floor, making the chore very difficult. It took several minutes for the task to be completed. Across the room, the sheriff appeared to hide a grin as he watched the battle.

Her eyes went back to the chair on her right. The man's chest heaved with each breath and large drops of rain dripped from the dark hair hiding his face.

Suddenly, his head snapped up, forcing the locks to flip back and making Jessie struggle to breathe. Eyes, more menacing than those of the Dodge City gunslinger Russell had hoodwinked, glared at each of the Quinter brothers. Skeeter, Bug, Hog, and Snake tripped over one another as they backed away from the man and the chair. His muffled words were unrecognizable, but the meanings made clear by the way the cloth over his mouth bulged. Jessie glanced to the trembling brothers, agreeing each needed to fear for their life.

The room became extremely quiet. Under her lashes, she snuck another peek at the man. The side of his face was red and swollen. A large gash, from his temple to the top of his cheek, oozed blood. She gasped. "Mrs. Quinter, this man is bleeding."

Stephanie Quinter rushed forward. The man tugged his head away from the woman's touch. "What did ya do to him?" Her voice sounded more harsh than usual. She hurried to the counter by the stove and snatched a piece of cloth. From a shelf above she gathered a few other items then scurried back to the table.

"Skeeter did it, Ma. I didn't," Bug said.

"He's wasn't gonna come, Ma. I had to knock him out." Skeeter defended his actions.

Stephanie started to wipe the blood away. The

man jerked again. "Hold still!" she instructed. His back became stiff in the chair, and his nostrils flared with each breath. "Did ya have to use a two-by-four?" the woman asked.

"Yeah!" Skeeter's eyes grew wide as he nodded his head.

The man's chair began hopping toward Skeeter and muffled words came out again. Stephanie tried to stop the chair. "Hold up there, Kid. I gotta get the bleeding to stop."

The breath in Jessie's lungs stilled. Kid? This was the man she had to marry? Beads of sweat broke out on her pounding forehead, and the room began to swirl. Bile churned in her stomach. She opened her mouth, searching for a breath of fresh air. It didn't help; the stuffy, stale air offered no relief. Every limb grew weak. The throbbing pain in her head faded as she slipped off the chair and a black void overtook her senses.

Kid tuned to the sound of a thud beside him. Reverend Kirkpatrick jumped from his chair and rushed to the body on the floor. The preacher rolled a girl onto her back. Kid glanced around the room. All eyes stared at the tiny body, his gaze copied theirs. Where had she come from?

"Now what did you do?" His mother looked to Skeeter.

"Nothing!" Skeeter lifted both hands in the air. "I didn't touch her. I swear!"

"Bug, get a pillow off my bed. Hog, get me a wet rag," she said. "Dang it, this is turning out to be more work than I imagined." While speaking, his mother ripped long strips of cloth and none to gently, wrapped them along the side of his face, under his chin and back up the other side of his face. Before she tied a knot on the top of his head she said, "I'm gonna take the gag off your mouth now Kid, but be quiet, I gotta tend to the girl."

Kid closed his eyes, wishing it were all a bad dream. Knowing it wasn't, he nodded in agreement and sucked in fresh air when the rag slipped away from his mouth. The bandana landed on the table, and she pulled the bandage tight. Several strands of hair caught in the strips of cloth. He ignored the sting as she twisted and tied the strands together. Simply one more ache among many.

What the hell were they up to this time? Once again, he looked toward the girl at his feet. Long, tangled hair spilled across the floor. The strands were a golden brown, like buffalo grass in July, not quite yellow, but not quite brown either. Her face was as white as a porcelain doll he'd seen at the mercantile in Dodge. The tiny body lay twisted, stretching thin material tightly across her bosom. The garment was worn thin, and the shoes on her feet had holes in the leather near the toes.

A feeling very similar to seeing a wounded animal, wafted through his chest. "Untie her hands," Kid demanded.

His mother flashed him a scowl.

"Now!"

She nodded and did as instructed before slipping a pillow beneath the tiny head. Hog handed their mother a wet rag. Kid gave him a hard stare as he stepped away to stand with the other brothers, near the door. All four looked ready to run. They damn well better, when he got out of these ropes he would beat each one into a bloody pulp.

"Is she all right?" a worried sounding voice asked from near the fireplace.

Kid turned and let his gaze float over the unfamiliar man. He glanced between the stranger and the girl. The man had hair the same color as the girl's. His skin was fair like hers and his eyes held a wide, questioning gaze. But his dapper three-piece suit was in much better condition than her clothes and the boots on his feet held the shine of new leather. Kid took an instant dislike to the man. "Who the hell are you?"

"I'm Russell Johnson." The man nodded his head to the girl. "She's my sister, Jessie."

The man's hands were tied behind his back as well. Kid turned toward his mother, his eyes catching those of Sheriff Turley on the way. The man nodded at him. Kid ignored it and asked Stephanie, "What the hell is going on?"

His mother wiped the wet cloth across the girl's cheeks and said, "I found this here girl to be your wife."

It felt as if his eyes popped clear out of their sockets. Air caught in his throat, and his mind went numb, incapable of thinking for a moment.

"She was supposed to be mine, but Ma said I couldn't have her," Skeeter complained.

Kid gave his brother a hateful stare. Skeeter hung his head in a pout. Shaking his head to clear his hearing, Kid took a deep breath and asked, "My what?"

"You need a wife. You can't keep rambling around in that big house by yourself. A good woman is what you need. This here one knows how to read and write. She knows her numbers, and is a pretty little thing. You'll see once she wakes up."

The top of his head felt as if it would explode. The young girl on the floor had to be a consequence to something his family had done. She was most likely nothing more than an innocent bystander. He turned to his brothers. "What have you four done now? I was only gone a week. A mere seven days!"

Chapter Three

Darkness began to clear. Loud, garbled voices filled her ears. Jessie twisted, trying to make out words, but there were too many, coming from all directions. A moan rumbled in her throat.

"Shush now! She's coming to," shouted above the others.

Jessie opened her eyes, recognizing Stephanie Quinter's rough voice. How'd she come to be lying on the floor? Her lids closed. *Please, please let it all be a dream.* She tugged them open again. Stephanie Quinter's face hovered inches above hers. Jessie covered both eyes with her hands. *So much for wishes and prayers.*

"There now sweetie, are you feeling better?" the woman asked.

Had her tone always sounded so kind and friendly? No, it had been harsh and forceful. The bite of the woman's voice was something Jessie clearly remembered. At least her hands were no longer tied. She pressed them against the floor.

With the help of the Reverend and Stephanie Quinter, Jessie rose to a sitting position. Confident the room was no longer spinning she nodded and allowed them to help her back into the chair. She settled onto the hard wood and twisted her hands in her lap. Rubbing at sore wrists, and unsure of the silence that had filled the room, she eased her gaze to the man sitting next to her.

Still tied to the chair, he now had several strips of white cloth wrapped around his face and tied atop his head with a wide bow. If she hadn't been so uncomfortable, she may have laughed at the sight.

He must have caught the glint of humor she was unable to hide. A gentle smile lifted the corners of his mouth and deep brown eyes sent a twinkle her way. His features were much softer than his brother's and held a hint of kindness. He shrugged his shoulders and shook his head. It reminded her of Russell's 'I'm sorry' look.

Her glance went to the fireplace. Russell still sat with his hands tied behind his back. Her fingers began to tremble. What had happened while she was out? She'd never fainted before in her life. The incident left her feeling more nervous, if that was possible.

"Miss Johnson, are you feeling all right?" The Reverend patted her shoulder.

"Y-yes, I'm fine. S-sorry for the, um, disruption," she murmured and lowered her gaze to the floor, realizing the entire room stared at her.

"Now that the medical emergencies are over, perhaps someone would care to tell me what's going on here?" the man beside her said.

Jessie didn't dare look his way. His voice didn't sound as friendly as his face had looked an instant ago. Silence hung in the air like dew in the morning. Refusing to allow her eyes to move from the shiny wood beneath her feet, she waited for the stillness to break. Her heart thudded so hard, she wondered if others could see the bodice of her gown jump with each rapid thump.

"Well?" he said.

Stephanie Quinter cleared her throat. "Like I told you, Kid, this here gal is ta be your wife. Reverend Kirkpatrick is here to perform the marriage."

His intake of breath whistled over his teeth. Jessie cringed, and afraid to breathe, waited for his outburst.

Kid Quinter's exhale was long and loud. It echoed through the silence of the room. Time ticked by a few minutes before, in a low, smooth voice, he asked, "How, may I ask, did this marriage come about?"

"Her brother here stole one of our horses. And since he no longer has it and can't return it, he agreed to give us his sister in exchange for not pressing charges," Stephanie Quinter explained.

Tears stung Jessie's eyes. Russell had pawned her off as a store clerk, a nanny, and a schoolteacher the past few years, but this was the first time he promised her as a wife. She blinked past the tears filling her eyes and snuck a peek at the man next to her.

His neck was bent backwards, the back of his head rested on the top rung of the chair. The wide, white bow fluttered as he took a deep breath. Slowly his head lifted. His dark brows furrowed and his gaze leveled on his brothers. "I think I need a few more details. Especially since none of you own a horse."

Hope made her eyes grow wide.

"We got a horse. Miss Molly. Or we had one anyway afore this thief stole her." Skeeter pointed to Russell.

"Miss Molly? That old nag's pushing thirty. She should've died years ago. That's the horse we're talking about?" Kid Quinter looked to the sheriff.

Sheriff Turley shrugged his shoulders. "A horse is a horse, and a horse thief is a horse thief." The lawman glanced to Russell. "In these parts, we hang horse thieves."

A lump formed in her throat. Jessie was mad at

her brother, but she didn't want to see him hanged. She looked at Kid Quinter. His gaze captured hers. She tried to pull away, but couldn't. He didn't blink, nor did the brown eyes flutter. They linked with hers. It felt like he could see into her mind and was reading each and every thought. He broke the contact by lowering lids that had thick, dark lashes.

Jessie pressed a hand to her chest, the thumping filled her palm.

When the lids lifted he looked at the youngest brother. "Bug, tell me the whole story."

"Alright, Kid." Bug shuffled his feet. "Uh-I met him in Nixon a few weeks ago." He pointed at Russell. "He was buying supplies and needed a ride home."

Jessie already questioned the tale. Russell never bought supplies, ever.

"And?" Kid Quinter lifted his eyebrows.

"The things he'd ordered weren't in, but I gave him a ride home. Well, almost home, I dropped him off near White Woman Creek. Then yesterday, he came by to see if he could buy a horse to go to town and pick up his order. Since all the horses here belong to you, I didn't dare sell him one of those, so I sold him Miss Molly. He said he'd be back with the money. Said he had to stop at the bank. He signed a bill of sale. Ma has it." Bug looked to his mother.

Stephanie Quinter laid a piece of paper on the table. Russell's fluent signature filled the bottom of the page.

"Fifty bucks? You sold Miss Molly for fifty bucks? She isn't worth fifty cents." Kid Quinter acknowledged the number above the signature.

"That's what I said. The nag didn't even make it to town. She collapsed and died before I got half way there. I told you I was swindled, Sheriff," Russell said.

"And I told you, Mr. Johnson, you can only be

swindled if money was actually exchanged. You admitted you didn't give Bug any money for the horse, nor do you have the fifty dollars you owe him. That makes you a horse thief," the sheriff said.

"She died?" the man beside her asked. His voice sounded deflated.

Russell nodded. "Yes!"

Kid Quinter turned to the sheriff. "Come on, Turley, you know Miss Molly wasn't worth fifty bucks."

"It doesn't matter how much she was worth. This man took her without paying for her. He can't return her, in the same condition she was when she left, nor can he pay for her. You know the law, Kid. This man either pays for Miss Molly or he hangs."

Jessie gasped and with shaky hands tried to wipe at the tears that had started to fall over her cheeks. All eyes in the room turned to her. She lowered her hands to her lap, wringing them together as the tears continued to trickle down her face. Whether they were because of the poor horse dying, or her brother's imminent hanging, she wasn't for sure, either way, she couldn't stop the water from slipping out of her eyes.

"If you don't want her, Kid, I'll marry her. Can't ya tell she don't want to see her brother hanged?" Skeeter's whinny voice penetrated her ears and caused a loud sob to burst between her lips. The skinny brother made her skin crawl.

"No, you won't," Stephanie Quinter piped in. "I already told you she's too fine for you. Had she been some sodbuster gal it would be different. Look at her, it's as plain as the nose on your face she's a refined gal. Knows her numbers and all, knows how to talk good. You wouldn't know what to do with her."

The woman's hands rubbed on Jessie's shoulders. She didn't know if she should be honored by the woman's kindness or frightened to death at the thought of marrying Kid Quinter. The one thing she did know, the older brother was a whole lot cleaner looking and acted kinder than Skeeter- if those were her only two choices. Unable to withstand the stares any longer, Jessie buried her face in her hands.

"Come on, Kid, the storm's lifted. I gotta get back to town. Either you agree to marry the girl, or I take her brother to town for hanging," Turley said.

Kid couldn't believe this was happening. Nor did he appreciate how much Malcolm Turley enjoyed it. The man had had it in for him for years. Since his cattle ranch became successful, the sheriff had gotten more determined. All because of Emma Sue White- the woman had once set her cap on him instead of the lofty sheriff. Kid gritted his teeth. To him it was water under the bridge. He hadn't had time for a wife back then and was glad when Turley finally married Emma Sue.

He still didn't have time for one. His attention went to the girl sitting next to him. It wasn't that she wasn't fine enough, matter of fact, she was a pretty little thing. His mother was right; the tiny gal was way too fine for Skeeter. He'd misuse the daylights out of her by just being in the same room. But he didn't want a wife, had no need for one. Not right now, he had too much to do with his ranch and keeping his four brothers and mother on the right side of the law. Besides, when he was ready to marry, he would go to Europe and bring back a refined English lady like the one Sam Wharton, the richest cattle baron west of the Mississippi, had married.

Kid shook his head, forcing his rambling thoughts to return to the present. The girl next to him trembled from head to toe, and tears fell from her eyes faster than she could wipe them away. Part of the reason he took to buying the frail cattle no one else wanted was because he couldn't stand the thought of someone misusing or destroying them. He knew with the right amount of care and nourishment, they'd become as strong and grand as the rest of the herd.

Those same feelings entered his chest. This little girl needed care and nourishment. Obviously, he was the only one who saw it; the rest of the room only saw fifty dollars or a hanging when they looked at her.

"What's it gonna be, Kid?" Turley's impatience was as clear as the Roman nose on his face.

"All right, I'll marry her."

The girl's head snapped toward him. He wasn't sure what he read on her face- thankfulness or fear. He wished his hands weren't still tied behind his back. He wanted to squeeze one of her tiny ones with reassurance. Let her know he'd never let any harm come to her. He'd nurture her until she was at her peak, and then... Then what? He'd have to think about what he'd do once she was fit for the world.

He pulled his eyes away and looked at her brother. "I'll marry her, under one condition."

"What's that?" Turley asked.

"That her brother comes to work for me. I'll pay him ten dollars a month, of which half will go to Bug to pay for Miss Molly. After ten months, when the debt is paid, the marriage will be dissolved."

The smile on Russell Johnson's face showed happiness with the arrangement. Kid let his gaze wander over the man. He recognized the shifty eye movements, the man's mind already scheming for a way to get out of the ten months of work. Kid felt a smile form, but didn't let it show. The man's hide had been saved, it was clear that was all he'd been concerned about. He showed little care to the harm he may have thrust on the sister. Well, it was time for Russell Johnson to learn a few lessons. The first one being Kid Quinter could not be swindled.

"That sounds fair to me," the sheriff said. "What do you think, Reverend?"

"Well, I don't believe in divorce, but under the circumstances, I could go along with the plan," Reverend Kirkpatrick agreed.

"Then start the service, Reverend," Stephanie Quinter said.

"Wait a minute, we don't need to have the ceremony right here, tonight," Kid said. He'd agreed to the event, but needed a bit more time to get used to it, to plan his next step of action.

"Yes, we do, Kid. If word got out a horse thief got away, I'd lose my job." Turley pointed to Kirkpatrick. "Go on Reverend."

"Could you at least untie me?" Kid asked.

Shuffling noises made Jessie turn to the brothers. They all scrambled for the door. Her fatigued mind, caught in a whirlwind, hadn't processed all that had been said. Had Kid Quinter agreed to marry her? She didn't know anything about being married, or how a marriage could be dissolved. And had he said Russell had to work for him? That could be worse than the marriage. Heavy dread bore down on her shoulders as the brothers fought over opening the door.

"No, I think not," Sheriff Turley said with a curt laugh. "I want to be well on my way back to town before you get untied." His glance landed on Jessie. "I don't want to have to arrest your husband for murder on your wedding night."

Her body went cold. The scuffling behind her ended and the sound of relieved sighs filled the room, making her shiver. Her gaze went to the man sitting beside her. Would he really kill his brothers? Would he kill Russell?

Never in her life had Jessie imagined she'd be

sitting at a table in a shanty in the middle of western Kansas marrying a man who was literally tied up from head to toe. Truth be told, she hadn't thought much about marriage, having always been too focused on finding food and shelter. She didn't have long to contemplate the thought nor what was going to happen next, because Reverend Kirkpatrick opened his Bible and began to read.

The ceremony took all of five minutes. The Reverend completed the session by saying, "I now pronounce you husband and wife." With a nod at the man sitting beside her, he continued, "You may now kiss the bride."

Kid Quinter tried to lean her way, but his bindings prevented any movement. All eyes were on them. Jessie had never kissed a man, nor had she ever been kissed, and had no idea what to do.

The Reverend cleared his throat. She looked up. His white-whiskered face and balding head tilted sideways as he stared down at her. Was he telling her to lean over so Kid could kiss her? Was that proper? The Reverend tilted his head again and pulled his eyes wide.

Without looking toward her new husband, she leaned sideways. Warm lips brush against her cheek, blistering the spot they touched. Gasping for breath, Jessie quickly pulled away and pressed a hand to the burning skin.

"This is just a suggestion, Kid, but I think Russell, should stay here at your Ma's place for a few days. He could start working for you the first part of next week. Give everyone time to adjust to the new situation," the sheriff said.

"Is there anything else you'd like to suggest, Turley?" Kid Quinter's eyes were little more than slits as he glared at the lawman.

"No, no, I think that about covers it." Sheriff Turley shook his head. "The Reverend and I are going to head home now." He looked toward the brothers. "Go get a wagon hitched up, we'll ride as far as Kid's house with you."

The brothers scrambled out the door in such a flurry they left it wide open. Cool, night air filled the room. Jessie took a deep breath, hoping it would clear her confused mind and calm her jumbled nerves. Was she really married? That's all it took- a few words from a preacher and a kiss on the cheek? She'd never dreamed of falling in love and living happily ever after, knew that wasn't a reality in the harsh, vast land of the west, but she'd always held a slight longing of finding someone she could care for, some one who'd care for her as they fought to survive their lot in life.

"There's no need for you to ride over to my place. It's out of your way. I assure you, I'm not going to harm them," Kid Quinter said.

The sheriff let out a low chuckle and walked across the room. "You must be forgetting how well I know you." He tipped the brim of his wide hat her way, then pulled the door shut as he walked out.

Blood pounded in her ears. She'd hoped Kid was the good brother, while Skeeter was the bad. But from what the sheriff implied, it appeared to be the other way around. Her gaze went to Russell. Eyes closed, his head rested on the back of the chair. He didn't appear to be at all concerned for her welfare. Many times over the past ten years she'd felt alone, but she'd never felt as lonely as she did at this moment. Tears pricked at her eyes again. She tried to buck up, to face this new adversity with courage, but her shoulders drooped, even valor had deserted her.

The door behind her flew open. Skeeter and Hog, or maybe it was Snake, the two looked a lot a like, walked in. "Ma, we'll bring your chair back," Skeeter said as they picked Kid up, chair and all, and carried him through the open door.

Stephanie Quinter walked over to the table. "You don't have anything to worry about, sweetie. Kid will be good to you. He's a good man, the best of the bunch." The woman's voice sounded soft and sincere.

Jessie didn't know how to respond. He may be the best of the bunch, but it was a very rough bunch.

Stephanie reached out and grasped her elbows, helping her rise. "You'll see," she said.

At that moment, Jessie wanted to lay her head on Stephanie Quinter's shoulder and cry her eyes out, but she couldn't. It would do little more than show how very vulnerable she felt. She blinked, hoping the woman didn't see the tears, and forced her head to nod in agreement.

"If you need anything, you just holler, and I'll be right there. I always wanted a daughter and feel right proud to be your ma," Stephanie said as she fluffed the long, tangled tresses falling over Jessie's shoulders. "Come on now, they're waiting for you."

Jessie told her feet to move, and with Stephanie's arm around her shoulder, she walked to the door. She wanted to turn to Russell and beg him to stand up for her, make it all go away, but that wasn't about to happen either. He didn't so much as whisper a good-bye as she left the house.

The rains had ended, leaving the air fresh and clean and the darkness of the night had lifted a touch. Faint streaks of light shimmered on the distant horizon. If only hope could rise with the morning sun, she might have something to look forward to.

Stephanie helped her climb into the back of the wagon. Kid, tied in the chair, sat near the front of the bed. The brothers had once again been thinking, not wanting him to tip over, they'd tied the chair to the seat of the wagon with another rope. Jessie sat down, then scooted a touch closer to his feet as Bug and either Hog or Snake, climbed in after her. Even tied up, his big frame oozed with authority and gave her a small safety net, which she gladly accepted. At this point, she'd take any protection she could get. Skeeter and the other brother sat in the driver's seat. Jessie swallowed and pressed a hand to the churning in her stomach.

"You boys come right home now, I'll be timing ya," Stephanie hollered as the wagon began to roll.

The sheriff made small talk from his horse beside the wagon as they began to ramble along. Jessie didn't try to listen. Too many thoughts already roamed her tired mind.

Using every ounce of his weight, Kid tried to keep the chair from bouncing. The loose ropes holding the chair legs to the wagon seat had him rocking in every direction. His brothers couldn't even tie right. There had to be a good hundred and fifty feet of rope wound around him, yet his wrists and ankles were the only things tied tight. He'd lost feeling in them some time ago.

Turley continued to rattle on. Kid made a comment in answer now and again, not really paying attention to the man. His eyes stayed focused on the woman huddled in front of him. He didn't want a chair leg to come down on one of her tiny feet. It wouldn't do any good to tell Skeeter to slow down; the ride was rough either way.

Thin arms wrapped around the bent knees pulled tight against her chest. Her chin bounced across her kneecaps as the wagon bounded over the rough terrain. An unbelievable amount of hair fluttered around her face and shoulders like the boughs of a weeping willow tree. He'd never seen so much hair and imagined it to be as soft as rabbit fur.

He leaned his head back and tried to gather his wandering thoughts. Streaks of morning light filtered the sky. A full day of work lie ahead sorting the cattle he'd brought back from Dodge. He sighed and brought his gaze back to the tiny creature. One cheek rested on the knees covered by the faded blue dress. The wind flipped the hair off the other, twisting the long tendrils as it blew past. Would she be safe at the house without him? The main reason he'd married her was because he knew if he didn't, one of his brothers would have, and no one deserved that type of torture.

Her clothes alone made it apparent the poor thing had been neglected the better part of her life. If only he could have stalled the ceremony, at least long enough to assure her everything would all be all right. But he damn sure couldn't do it in front of his brothers or Turley, no reason on earth would make him display that kind of compassion in front of them. They'd use it against him. Letting them all think he was a hard ass was much better, normally it guaranteed he had the upper hand.

The wagon slowed a mite, taking the corner around calving pens and down the road to the house. Kid sat up straight and pressed his weight onto the chair, preparing for the sudden halt. As usual, Skeeter brought the wagon to a stop so abrupt everyone bounded about. The girl fell against his legs. Jessie, he had to try and think of her as Jessie instead of the girl.

"Sorry," she murmured and righted her body.

"Couldn't be helped. Skeeter hasn't learned how to drive yet," he said. "If this chair wasn't tied down I'd have flown out."

There was enough light to see a slight smile cross her face. It was a delightful sight, one that tugged at his heart. Poor little thing, she'd probably had a nastier night than he. He knew first hand how frightening his brothers and mother could be when they set their minds to it.

The boys tugged, twisted, and pulled to the point Kid seriously considered doing each of them bodily harm when he was finally cut loose. Jarred until even his teeth ached; they eventually sat his bound frame onto the top step of the front porch. He squirmed against the ropes, and keeping his balance by planting his boots on the wood of the stairs below, glared at the boys.

"None of this was my idea, Kid. Please don't be mad at me," Bug said.

"I'm disappointed in you, Bug. You have to start thinking for yourself," Kid said, keeping his voice low so only the youngest brother could hear it.

Bug hung his head and kicked at the dirt as he followed the other three to the wagon. Regret made Kid lower his head. He hadn't meant to make Bug feel bad, but someone had to give the boy direction.

"Ma'am." The scratchy sound of Turley's voice made his head snapped back up. From the back of his horse, the joke of a sheriff instructed, "I think it would be best if you waited half an hour or so before you untie him. Give the boys here a head start."

Jessie stood at the base of the steps, a worried frown on her lips. Her eyes flashed nervously between him and the sheriff.

"I think it would be best if you all stayed away from my place for at least a week," Kid growled. Let them all think he wanted to murder them. He could use the peace and quiet after tonight.

Sammy's non-stop barking filtered through the door behind him. Turley turned to Jessie again. "Please don't let that dog out until we're out of sight either."

Her eyes grew wide. Damn it. The man was trying to scare her. "Get the hell out of here, all of you!" Kid shouted.

Turley's chuckle echoed in the morning air as he, the Reverend, and the wagon full of his brothers turned to leave the yard.

Kid waited until the dust behind them began to settle before he said, "He's just trying to frighten you. Sammy wouldn't hurt anyone. Well, he won't hurt you. Can't say what he might do to some of the boys. A couple of them picked on him when he was a pup, and he's never forgotten it."

"I-I've never been around dogs. I've seen them here and there, but..." She shuffled her feet, her voice so low he could barely hear it.

He smiled and said, "Come here."

Chapter Four

Kid half expected her to turn and run, fleeing as far from the ranch as she could. Instead, tiny and cautious steps climbed the five stairs to where he sat on the porch. "Untie me and I'll introduce you to Sammy. He's a good dog," he said when she stopped to stand beside him, trembling from head to toe.

"The, um, um, sheriff said I was supposed to wait." Her tiny fingers twisted about until they were wrung together.

"I know what Turley said, but I'm not going to go after them." She reminded him of a tiny, orphan calf- afraid, alone, and in need of care.

Weary, pale blue eyes looked at him. "You're not?"

"No." He shook his head and hoping to ease her fears, explained, "First off, my legs have been tied together for so long it's going to hurt like hell to walk. Second, I'm tired, and my head hurts too bad to confront the boys right now. And third, they aren't worth it."

Those eyes, the color of a robin's egg, squinted, causing tiny lines to track across her forehead. "They aren't worth it?" she asked, disbelief lacing her voice.

Kid let out a loud sigh. "As awful as this may seem to you, this is nothing compared to some of the other stunts the boys have pulled. And Turley's just trying to scare you. He makes a good sheriff because he's a bully. Always has been."

She crouched near his feet and began to tug on the knots. "Really?"

"Yeah, really. He likes bullying people around."

"No, I mean your brothers have done things worse than they did tonight?"

"Believe it or not, yes." He nodded and gave her what he hoped was a reassuring smile. "Lift up my left pant leg. There's a knife on the side of my boot, use it to cut the ropes. One of the only things Skeeter can do is tie a good knot."

Jessie did as instructed. He twisted his ankles against the sting as the ropes fell away. She moved to his back and released the ropes on his wrists, then started to cut the many strands around his arms and chest. The bindings fell away. "Ah, it feels like I've just been sprung from jail. Here, give me the knife, I'll get the ones around my knees."

When the last rope fell away, he slipped the knife back into its leather holder, rose to his feet, and stepped away from the mass of jute. No wonder he thought of her as a girl, the top of her head didn't even come up to his shoulders. He smiled down at the cherub face looking up. Not quite sure what else to do, he held out a hand. "Hello Jessie, I'm Kid Quinter, nice to meet you."

A guarded smile touched her cheeks as a tiny giggle escaped her lips. She put her hand in his. "Hello, Kid Quinter, I'm happy to meet you, too."

His large hand engulfed her tiny one. The little fingertips were ice cold. Kid tightened his hold, hoping his warm palm would send heat into hers. "Happy are you?"

Her face pulled into a grimace. "Considering the rest of your brothers, yes, I'm happy to meet you."

Kid threw his head back and laughed. A deep, full laugh that felt good. "I think that's one of the most honest things I've ever heard, Jessie. Thank you."

"You're welcome," she said, her voice sounding stronger than it had all night.

Kid pulled her hand. "Come on, I gotta let Sammy out before he knocks the door down." He led her across the porch. "Like I said, he's a good dog. You just have to let him know who the boss is. He has the boys buffaloed into believing he's a killer, and I don't see a reason to change their way of thinking." He pushed the door open, turned to the dog, and said, "Sammy, sit," before he tugged Jessie into the house.

His hand, warm and big, pulled, leaving Jessie no choice but to follow. She stepped over the threshold and froze. It was big, black, and huge, white fangs stuck out below a long nose. The perfect image she had of the wolves she often heard howling deep in the night. A low growled filled the air. Without a second thought, she jumped sideways, hiding herself behind Kid's back. Her knees knocked together like a hammer on a nail head.

The material of his shirt rubbed against her cheek as his shoulder blade moved up and down and the rumble of his chuckle filled her ear before he said, "Sammy, you scared her. Come here, be a good dog and say hello to Jessie."

She didn't want to move, but Kid had a hold of her hand, and he used it to haul her out of hiding. Swallowing the lump in her throat, she went, but wasn't in the least eager to face the beast. He knelt down to pat the dog on the head. A bushy tail thumped against the floor. Her hand, pulled by his, brushed against the tip of the dog's nose. Nostrils flared as they sniffed her skin. If Kid hadn't held her hand still, she would have pulled it back, away from the wet nose.

"She's going to be living here, you better be nice

to her or you'll answer to me," Kid said.

Her gaze went from the dog to the man kneeling beside her. The huge bandage tied around his head made him look like a little boy, and pulled her thoughts away from the big dog for a moment. A smiled tugged at the sides of her lips.

"What?" he said.

"What, what?" she asked.

"You're staring at me. No, you're laughing at me." Dark brows pulled together as his hand went to the top of his head. He patted the white strips of cloth. "Ah, shit, don't tell me she tied it with a big, billowing bow."

Jessie nodded. A giggle escaped her lips. She clamped her mouth shut, fearful of offending him.

Kid chuckled. One of his dark eyes winked. "I bet it looks real good."

A warm, silly feeling crept into her cheeks. She couldn't help but smile and nod in agreement.

The hand still holding hers tightened, sending something balmy and tingly to flow up her arm. The sun, rising over the horizon, streamed in through the open front door to land on them. She felt it on her face and saw it on his. During the ride home the wind had twisted his hair here and there around the bandage. It was dark, not black, but a deep shade of brown. Several strands clumped together to fall over his forehead. Her heart skipped a beat. Even sporting a big, white bow, he was certainly the most handsome man she'd ever seen.

Something hit her leg and uprooted her balance. Rocking, she stepped sideways, trying to keep from tumbling. Kid's other hand clamped onto her waist, steadying her balance. He glanced at the dog.

"Sammy! Sit!"

Jessie felt funny- all warm and tingly. *Must be the morning sun.* She squeezed her eyes shut. Or maybe it was because she hadn't had any sleep.

A finger touched the skin below her chin, lifting it up.

"Sorry, he just wanted to say hello," Kid said.

She blinked several times, trying to determine what the smile on his face meant, before turning to the dog to whisper, "Hello, Sammy."

Kid let go of her hand. "Go ahead, he won't bite you."

Somewhat apprehensive, Jessie let her fingers brush against the top of the dog's wide head. It tilted sideways, and she gently scratched the soft hair behind the wide, floppy ears. Big, brown eyes looked at her, and the dog leaned closer, his flank touching the side of her dress.

"He likes you. You'll have a friend forever now," Kid said.

Her heart felt warm- something she hadn't felt in a very long time. She kept her eyes on the dog. "I hope so. I really hope so." Her hand ran over the wide head and along his sleek back. She could use a friend, even a non-human one was better than what she had.

After a few minutes Kid said, "All right Sammy, that's enough, time for you to go out."

The dog whimpered and looked at her with big, droopy eyes, as if asking if he had to listen to Kid.

Kid laughed. "Nice try, old man. Out, now." His hand left her hip and pointed to the door.

The spot were his hand had been instantly felt chilled, and she hoped he didn't notice the slight quiver that rippled her body. She didn't dare meet his eyes.

Sammy stood and tossing a nasty glance at Kid, slowly walked to the front porch. Kid followed and almost caught the dog's tail as he closed the door. After it clicked shut, he turned around. "Well, I guess this is your new home." He pointed to the area where she stood. "This is the front room. I-ah, don't use it much."

Jessie glanced around and almost gasped. How had the elegance and size of the house escaped her notice? A massive stone fireplace covered the furthest wall. A tapestry divan and two leather side chairs sat in front of it. Other chairs and tables sat along the walls, and near the door behind him stood a tall coat rack. The center of it held a large mirror, and the wood frame had hooks on which two hats and a jacket hung. Near the bottom of the rack was a bench to sit on while taking off or putting on shoes. She'd remembered seeing one just like it in a catalog years ago and had begged her father to buy it. He'd promised someday she would have one.

Kid pointed behind her. "Upstairs there are six bedrooms, one's mine of course, but you can have your pick of the other five. Down the hall behind the staircase are my office and another room I use for storage. Over there," he pointed to her left, "is the kitchen."

Her eyes followed his verbal tour. The staircase was wide and made a sweeping motion as it rose to the second floor. The spindled banister followed the steps to the top where it ran along an open area before merging into the wall with natural flow. She could imagine standing up there and watching him walk in through the front door. The thought made her cheeks burn. At the bottom of the stairs, sunlight glistened through a tall window at the end of the long hall. Brass door knobs on each side of the hallway shined in the light.

Her eyes floated past the archway that led into the area he pointed to as the kitchen and landed on etched glass doors beside it. Swung wide, the doors led to a room with a large table, at least a dozen chairs, and a huge buffet full of sparkling china.

"Oh, that's the dining room. I've never used it," Kid explained.

"It's beautiful," she whispered. The house was just like the one she dreamed of, especially on long, cold nights when she'd had no roof over her head. Funny, she dreamt of the home she wanted, but never the family she wanted to live in it with her.

"Thank you. Ma and the boys think it's too big. But I wanted a big house, just like the one I used to live in in Missouri."

"You lived in Missouri? So did I." A twinge of homesickness touched her heart. "Where at in Missouri?"

"St. Louis, what about you?"

"Independence."

He nodded and started to walk toward the kitchen. "I'm going to make some coffee, would you like some?" Stopping, he made a sweeping motion for her to follow.

Jessie walked to where he stood in the kitchen archway. She stumbled, once again in awe. Kid's hand touched the small of her back. She jumped, mumbling, "Sorry," and moved forward. "How- why..." Jessie wasn't sure what she wanted to ask.

"Why do I have such a nice place while my family lives in a shanty?" Kid walked around her. "It's called choices, Jessie. We all have choices to make. We can't always choose the things that happen in our lives, but we can choose how we react to them."

"What do you mean- choices?" She followed as he walked to the stove.

"Have a seat, and I'll explain." He dumped a handful of beans into a grinder.

She looked at the table. It was long and wide, the wood sanded smooth and coated with varnish. Six matching chairs sat around it. A great contrast to the rough-hewn table and chair at her soddy. The thought made her mind snap. She wouldn't be returning to the sod house. A frown formed as she turned to where he stood near the wide counter. If she was the wife, she should be the one making coffee, not him. Shouldn't she? Realizing how little she knew about being married made her stomach flip.

Pressing against the sensation with one hand, she glanced back to the table and quickly decided not to sit. Instead, she walked over and took the coffee pot from the stove then went to the large stone crock sitting by the door. The coffee grinder filled the room with sound, her eyes asked if it was the water she was to use. He nodded. With a dipper, she filled the pot and carried it back to him.

"Thank you." He took the pot and bent to light a fire in the bin of the stove.

She handed him two sticks of wood from the box next to the stove and said, "I could change your bandage while you tell me what you mean about choices."

"I don't know, do you think you can make a bandage look as good as this one?" His eyes held a teasing glimmer as he rose to stand beside her.

"Probably not." She shrugged, smiling at his mockery.

"Good," he laughed, walked to the table, and sat in a chair.

The sound made something in her insides flutter. She ignored it, and careful not to pull his hair while untying the bandage, asked, "What do you mean choices in how we react?" The material let loose, and she began to unwind it from around his head.

"Well, for instance, look at the situation we have found ourselves in. We have a choice of how to react to this uh, marriage. We could both be angry with our families and sit here and plot our revenge. Or we can look at it as an opportunity to make our lives better, despite their actions." The last of the bandage fell from his cheek, and he turned to look up at her.

Jessie didn't meet his gaze, choosing instead to let his words sink in while she gathered the strips of cloth. "Your mother's bandage may not have looked the best, but it did the job. The cut isn't bleeding. Actually, it doesn't look as bad as I expected."

"Really?" He stood and strolled across the room to a door on the far wall. Opening it, he walked into the area.

Still mulling over his statement, but curious, Jessie followed and peeked through the open doorway. Two windows filled the room with light. A large brass tub, a bench, and a washstand with bowl and mirror furnished the room.

His head twisted sideways as he examined the cut in the mirror. "You're right it's not as bad as I expected either." He poured water from the pitcher into the bowl, cupped it in his hands and began to splash his face.

Jessie backed out of the opening. *A washroom!* She'd heard some homes had them, but had never seen one. Her mind fluttered, there was too much to think about at once. She walked to the stove and checked the coffee. The rich aroma made her stomach growl.

"Cups are over there." Kid stepped out of the room and pointed to a cupboard on her left. "Pour me one too, please." He opened another cupboard, took out a container, and held it up. "It's a balm Stephanie makes. It's good for man or beast."

Unsure how to answer, she nodded, opened a hinged door, and stared at the stacks of dishes. After years of living with the barest of essentials, the abundance of the house overwhelmed her senses. Kid Quinter overwhelmed her senses, so did the dog, the marriage; actually everything about the night beset her. She blinked at the sting in her eyes, sucked in a gulp of air then pulled two cups off the shelf. After filling them, she set them on the table.

Kid finished smoothing the balm over his cheek, replaced the container then walked to the table. "Sit down." He pointed to the chair in front of her as he sat down at the end of the table next to her.

She pulled out the chair, but her wondering mind was no longer able to keep silent. "What do you mean, an opportunity to make our lives better?" she asked, pressing a hand to the racing in her chest. Dare she hope this escapade could turn out to be a blessing?

Kid took a sip of the hot coffee. It tasted like heaven, and he needed the pep it would give him. He was dog tired, his head hurt, in fact, most of his body hurt from the rough treatment he'd had the past several hours, and he had a full day of work ahead of him. He took another sip and looked over the rim at the young girl.

She sniffed at the contents of the cup before taking a small drink. Her face puckered as she swallowed. A chuckle tickled his throat.

"I like my coffee a bit strong." He went to the icebox and pulled out the pitcher of milk. "This will help." A dollop turned the liquid in her cup light tan. "Try that."

She blew into the cup before taking a sip. "Mmm, much better, thank you." The tip of a pink tongue licked her lips before she took another drink. "So, what did you mean?"

"What I said, we have a choice. We can focus on how awful it was of our families to do this to us, and dwell on it, and them. Or we can see the good that could come out of it, and focus on that."

"The good?" Tiny lines laced across her forehead again.

"Yes, the good." He poured more coffee into their cups, watching the changes her face made as her mind contemplated his words.

She added milk to hers, but didn't take a drink right away. Her eyes fluttered around the room, and her top teeth bit down on her bottom lip. Tiny fingers tapped the side of her cup.

Kid waited for her to speak. When his cup was half empty, he couldn't wait any longer. "What are you thinking so hard about?"

Her face took on a sad, almost painful look. "Well, wh-what does the good all entitle?"

Kid couldn't help but tease her a bit. With a mocked serious look, he said, "That we get to know each other."

Her eyes went to her cup. "H-how well?"

He had to laugh, couldn't hold it in, and reached over to pat her hand. "Jessie, you'll never have a reason to fear me. I promise. We'll get to know each other as friends. Not as husband and wife. I don't have time for a wife right now." He really didn't have time for a friend either, not one that needed as much as she apparently did, but it was too late to dwell on that now.

"You don't have time for a wife?" She pulled her fingers out from beneath his and wrapped them around the cup, using both hands to lift it to her lips. "I'd have thought you'd want a wife to help you. This is a big house to take care of, besides all of your ranching."

"I don't use much of the house except the kitchen and my bedroom, so the upkeep isn't much. And I pay Stephanie to come and give it a good cleaning every once in awhile."

"Why do you call your mother Stephanie?"

"Because she's not my mother. My mother died when I was five." Kid pushed away from the table, needing something to occupy his hands, they itched to touch hers again. "Are you hungry?"

"N-no, I'm fine. The coffee is good."

"Well, I am." He moved around the kitchen,

placing a pan on the stove, and gathering eggs from the basket on the other end of the counter. He didn't mind sharing the story of his life and talked while he worked.

"We lived in St. Louis. She and the baby died. I don't really know what happened, since no one ever talked about it. One day she was there, the next she wasn't." He cracked a few eggs into the pan. "One day, my dad was gone too. I lived with an aunt and uncle until I was ten. Then out of the blue, my father showed up and brought me out here. That's when I met my new stepmother and brother. Skeeter wasn't much more than a baby, two or so, and Stephanie was pregnant with Snake."

It had been a long time since he'd thought about his younger days. Kid flipped the eggs and listened to them sizzle for a minute. "There's some bread and jam in that cupboard if you'd like some with your eggs."

"Oh, oh, I'm sorry." Jessie jumped from the table and scurried to the cupboard.

"There's nothing to be sorry about. I just thought you might like some," Kid said. She moved about quickly, gathering the bread and jam while he piled the fried eggs on two plates. A smile formed, sharing a meal with someone was nice.

"It was like that with my parents too. Like you said, one day they were there, the next they were gone." She found silverware and glasses and carried them to the table.

"How did they die?" Kid set the plates on the table.

"Cholera."

"Heard of that. Bad news." He motioned for her to sit. "How old were you?"

She smoothed the worn material over her knees after taking a seat. "Eight when they died, it was ten years ago," she said, a lonely little sigh escaping her lips after the words.

Kid sat, picked up his fork, and began to eat. That would make her eighteen, older than he thought. He'd have guessed sixteen at the most.

Looking between him and the food, she asked, "There's something I hope you don't mind my asking about."

It must be serious. Kid laid his fork down and nodded. "Of course I don't mind. Ask whatever you want."

"Well, it's about your- your brother's names." Her face puckered into that painful look again. "There a little, um, odd?"

Kid laughed. "Yeah, they are. Our dad did that."

"Named you?"

"Well, gave us all nicknames. My name is Kendell, but Dad always called me the kid. He said Skeeter was as pesky as a mosquito. His real name is Steven. Snake-as sneaky as a Snake, is Scott. Hog, 'cause he grunts like one is Howard, and Bug, because he was as cute as a bug in a rug, is Brett."

"Oh. Kendell?"

"Yes, after my mother's father."

"And Steven, Scott, Howard and Brett."

"Yup, the Quinter boys," he said.

"Jessie is a nickname too," she admitted.

"Oh? What's your real name?" he asked.

"Jessica," she said.

He didn't reply because a knock sounded on the door and made him realize how late in the morning it already was. "Come in, Joe." Kid waved his hand at the man peeking in the window of the back door while scooping up the last of his eggs with his fork.

"Mornin', Kid."

Jessie turned to the sound behind her. A tall, thin, older man closed the door behind him. He turned her way and his feet froze mid-step.

"Ah, um, oh, well..."

"Grab a cup of coffee, Joe." Kid mopped a piece of bread across his plate.

"I can get him one," Jessie said, somewhat anxious to move out of the newcomer's shocked stare. She put a hand on the table to rise.

Kid covered it with one of his. "No, finish your breakfast."

"I did." A warm flush filled her cheeks at how she'd gobbled the eggs and bread.

"Then finish your coffee."

"I did."

"Joe, bring the pot to the table, will ya?"

"Sure," the man said. His gaze kept bouncing to her, and he almost slopped the coffee on Kid when he attempted to refill the cups on the table.

Kid took the pot and refilled his and her cups while the other man sat down across the table from her. "Joe, this is Jessie. Jessie, this is Joe. He's the foreman here at the ranch."

"Ma'am." Joe touched the brim of his hat. Then his cheeks turned pink, and he took the head covering off and laid it on the floor by his feet.

"Hello." Jessie had no idea what to say. Or do. She folded her hands in her lap.

"Jessie and I were married last night." Kid nonchalantly lifted his cup to his lips. As if he'd just said the sun was shining today.

Jessie gasped and before she could turn to stare at Kid, coffee shot out of Joe's mouth. It spewed across the table as he started coughing.

Kid rose to pound the other man on the back. "Not what you expected?" Kid asked when Joe's coughing ended.

Jessie retrieved two dishtowels near the sink. She handed one to Joe and used the other to wipe the table. Her gaze went to Kid. He grinned from ear to ear. It made her want to smile, and she wasn't quite sure why.

"That wasn't very nice," she whispered, glancing to see if Joe was all right.

Kid laughed aloud.

Joe, with a frown between his brows, looked between her and Kid. "Oh, so it's a joke. You really caught me off guard." He refilled his cup and lifted it to his mouth again.

"No, it's not a joke. We really did get married last night," Kid said.

This time Joe swallowed before he started to cough. He set the cup down and glanced at Jessie.

Kid stepped over to stand beside her. His arm circled her shoulders, and he smiled down at her. She didn't know what to think of the grin, nor the arm. Her heart began thumping.

"Really?" Joe asked. His stare stuck on her.

Hoping her face didn't show the confusion she felt, she attempted a smile and nodded.

"Holy shit!" Joe's face turned beet red. "Oh, sorry, I mean, excuse me, Ma'am."

Kid's hand slipped away and needing something to do, Jessie leaned over to remove their breakfast clutter from the table. Forcing her fingers not to tremble, she picked up her used silverware, setting it upon the empty plate.

"Did you spend the night with the herd?" Kid sat down and poured another cup of coffee.

"Yeah," Joe said. "Are you really married?"

"Yeah." Kid smiled at her as she picked up his plate, and then glanced back to Joe. "How'd the herd weather the storm?"

She twisted and walked toward the sink with the dishes. The feeling wafting every inch of her body wasn't what she'd call embarrassment, and it certainly couldn't be called happiness. Taking a deep breath, she quit trying to analyze unexplainable emotions and listened instead.

"Fine," Joe said. "When, where, how?"

"At my mother's- about four or so this morning. No stampedes with all the lightning?"

Jessie snuck a peek their way.

"No." Joe shook his head. "Was it planned?"

"No." Kid took another swallow of coffee. "Any strikes near?"

"No. A few way off, nothing close." Joe's pause was slight. "How?"

"The regular way, with a preacher. Are the rest of the boys still out there?"

Jessie set the dishes on the counter, her mind weary from trying to follow their conversation. Goose bumps rose on her arms, wondering what else Kid would say about their marriage. She twisted toward the table, rubbing at the cold tingles, and waited.

"Yes, the rest of the boys are still out there. I rode in to see where you were. You're over an hour late. We thought something might have happened." Joe set his cup down and looked at Jessie. "I guess something did."

"Yes, something did." Kid also looked her way.

Both men were silent, their gazes floating over her. Self conscious, her hands went to her hair. She must look a mess. Between the wind and the rain, the unruly mass probably looked like a bird's nest. Her fingers caught on long, snarled strands. Embarrassed, she flipped around and covered her face with both hands.

"I'll meet you outside in a few minutes, Joe," Kid said. Within seconds, the sound of a door closing echoed in the room and large hands fell on her shoulders. The heat of his fingers penetrated through the material of her dress as they gently massaged her tight muscles. "Are you all right?" he asked.

She nodded.

The pressure on her shoulders increased and forced her to turn toward him. "You must be tired.

Let me show you to one of the rooms upstairs."

"No, if I go to sleep now, I may sleep all day." She glanced around, trying to find something to focus on, anything except his face.

His hands touched her cheeks, making her look at him. "And what would be wrong with that?"

"Well, well, I can't sleep the day away. There must be chores around here for me to do."

"Not really."

"The dishes, I could do the dishes, and sweep the floors, and you must have laundry..."

Kid's arm was around her shoulder again. The feeling was so gentle, so kind, she had to swallow a sob forming in her throat.

With slight pressure, he forced her to walk across the kitchen beside him. "Maybe tomorrow you'll feel up to doing some of those chores. But for today, I think a good sleep is in order."

"I couldn't sleep right now."

"I think you could, and I think you will." Kid stopped every protest she tried to make as he led her through the house and up the stairs. He pushed open a door, and the beauty of the room made her gasp again, her tired mind incapable of taking in much more.

Kid patted her upper arm. "You are not allowed downstairs until after you've rested. Understand?"

Part of her wondered what would happen if she disobeyed. Would she see the wrath the sheriff talked about and his brothers feared? The other part of her was too exhausted to think any longer. "Y-yes," she murmured, and when he left the room, thankfully fell onto the bed covered with a flower print quilt.

Chapter Five

Hours later, Kid pulled the hat from his head and let it fall to the ground. Cupping his hands, he splashed a few handfuls of water from the horse trough on his face. It was lukewarm, but refreshing nonetheless. One cheek stung, he ignored it and wiped the water from his face, pushing the droplets back to mingle with the sweat in his hair then bent to retrieve his hat. He forced the dust from the rim by slapping it against his knee before pushing it onto his wet hair.

Faint light from the setting sun bounced off the glass panes of the ranch house. Joe said Jessie was still in there, had only ventured outside a couple times during the day. He'd asked the foreman to work at the homestead today, assuring she wouldn't be alone in case his brothers came sneaking around. He was pretty sure they wouldn't, but didn't know about Russell. The man's inability to care for his little sister really irritated him. After seeing the sod shanty she'd been living in, he was even more annoyed.

This morning after telling Joe to stay about the house, he'd gone out and helped the cowboys separate the livestock. Once the task was completed, he'd instructed the boys where to drive each group then rode over to gather some of Jessie's belongings, knowing she'd need a few things. What he'd found was disheartening. No one could possibly live in that soddy. He'd heard the hissing of snakes before dismounting Jack.

Luckily, they were only bull snakes. The storm had sent a dozen or so into the shack. And it hadn't been the first time. Holes along the base of the entire structure showed the reptiles had used it as a shelter for some time.

The inside, though neat as possible, had puddles deep enough for frogs to live in and the storm had ripped the weathered shutters from the one window. Rain had completely soaked the worn quilt of the only bed. He'd searched high and low for clothes and personal belongings, but found nothing other than the silver handle hair brush in his back pocket.

The only other salvageable things were the small table and one crudely built chair. He had no use for either and left them behind, after he released the three grouse that had somehow managed to trap themselves in a small wooden pen. If the birds were a bit smarter they would have realized they could have easily flown over the low sides of the haphazard enclosure. He shuddered at the thought of anyone, even prairie chickens, living in such conditions.

Sammy's bark emitted from the back door. The sound forced Kid to make his way toward the house, knowing the dog had alerted Jessie to his arrival. Thick mud from traipsing through the soddy had gathered on the bottom of his boots. He knocked it off on the rock near the steps before climbing the porch stairs and opening the door.

The smell of scorched food made his nose and throat sting. Black smoke billowed from the oven door. Jessie stood beside the stove, waving a cloth at the swirls. He hurried across the room, grabbed the cloth from her hands and used it to remove the pan from the oven. Coughing at the acrid smoke, he carried the unrecognizable charred mass out the door. After setting the hot container on the ground, he waved the smoke away from his face and gulped for fresh air. Whatever was in the pan continued to crackle and hiss as he turned to walk back to the house.

Jessie stood on the porch, wringing her hands together. "Oh, Mr. Quinter, I'm so sorry. I've never used an oven before. I thought I could bake some biscuits for supper. I..."

"Those were biscuits?"

She nodded. "I thought I just smelled the wood burning, until I opened the oven door." Her face scrunched with a worried frown.

"Did you burn yourself?"

"No, Sir." She glanced down at her hands, inspecting them.

Kid reached out and took the small fingers into his, looking for red marks. The tiny digits trembled, each one shivering in his palms. His gaze rose up her arms, past the slender neck to the top of her head. The long tresses had been smoothed away from her face and fell behind her shoulders like a cascade of corn silk. The flush on her round, elfin cheeks once again reminded him of a china doll. His fingers itched to see if the flawless skin felt as smooth and soft as it looked.

The long, curled lashes of her lids fluttered up and down, making it hard for him to connect with the unique blue of her eyes. Then he caught the moisture on the tips of the lashes. The tears melted his heart. He brushed one thumb over the wetness. "Don't cry over burnt biscuits, Jessie."

The flutters stopped and her gaze met his. "I...I wanted to have supper ready when you got home."

Yup, his heart was melting, warm, thick, blood raced to fill every inch of his six feet height. He squeezed the hand still in his and used his other to turn her around, toward the door. Guiding her beside him, he smiled down on the face looking up at him. "Thank you for trying. That was very nice of you."

The haze had cleared, but the smell of burnt biscuits still filled the kitchen. Her pert nose curled up, and a sweet, soft smiled covered her face. "The stew should still be fine." She slipped from beneath his arm, walked to the stove and lifted the lid off a pot.

The separation came too quickly, he reached a hand out, almost grabbing her fleeing form before he realized the movement and shoved his hands in his pockets.

"I'm sure it will be fine. I'm so hungry I could eat a horse." Kid walked to the table. Maybe having a wife wouldn't be so bad, he wasn't much of a cook, but had managed to get by. A hot meal waiting every evening, as well as the company of a welcoming face would be a comfort he hadn't had in years.

Jessie carried two bowls to the table, set one in front of him, and sat down. He looked at the dark broth in the bowl. A frown tugged at his brows. Steam floated up from it and tried to penetrate his nostrils. He sniffed harder. His sense of smell must still be irritated from the smoke, because he couldn't catch an appetizing whiff. It smelled more like old jerky.

He lifted his spoon and stirred the contents. In the bottom of the bowl of brown water he detected a chunk of something. Catching it with the spoon, he lifted it into view. It looked like a chunk of old jerky. He glanced at Jessie.

She lifted a spoonful, blew on it, and let the soup pour between her lips. Her tongue came out to catch any leftover drips before the spoon went back into the bowl.

Kid let the chunk fall back into the bowl and

filled the spoon with broth. The hot liquid landed in his mouth. Quickly, he pulled the spoon out and fought to swallow the bitter brew. His gag reflex put up a good fight. With a painful swallow, he managed to win the battle.

She continued to eat the soup like it was quite delicious. Her little tongue licked across pink lips with each sip. He pulled his gaze from the enticing picture and tried a second spoonful. This one was harder to make go down than the first one had been. It tasted like water old jerky had been boiled in. He searched for the clump in his bowl again, and once he found it, lifted it out. It was an old chunk of jerky.

Sparkling blue eyes gazed at him, her smile encouraging him to eat. He gave a slight nod, and hiding a shudder, regrettably slipped the spoon into his mouth. His jaw tightened as he chewed. And chewed...and chewed, trying to break down the smoked meat.

When Jessie looked back down at her bowl, as discreet as possible, he pulled the meat from his mouth and slipped it beneath the table.

A soft whine let him know Sammy wasn't willing to take it from his fingers. Stupid dog, he eats anything- everything. He glanced down and waved it below the dog's nose. Sammy lowered to the floor and placed both paws over his long snout.

Disgusted by the mutt, he pushed his chair away from the table. "Come on Sammy, you can go out while we eat." He walked to the door.

Sammy looked from him to Jessie. She reached down and patted the dog's head. "Be a good dog and go outside now."

The lab gave him a scowl before he rose to his feet and padded to the door. After Sammy meandered out, Kid threw the chunk of meat out the door and closed it. He walked over to the cupboard and took out a loaf of bread, sliced off several large pieces, found a jar of his mother's jam, and carried it all to the table. Evidently, his new wife didn't know how to cook. Still, he looked forward to her company.

Jessie accepted the piece he handed her. "Thank you. Would you like some more stew?"

"No, no, thank you. This will be fine." He pretended to eat a few more mouthfuls of soup before he gave up and filled the empty pit in his stomach with slices of bread. A new thought formed. "Did you find the pantry today?"

"The pantry?"

"Yes, the door, over there, beyond the stove, that's the pantry. There should be most everything you need for cooking in there. And behind the house, the small mound with the door, that's the root cellar. It has more supplies, as well as the ice for the ice box."

"Oh, no, I didn't look in either place. I found this jerky in the saddle bags on the coat rack by the front door, so thought I'd make a stew from it. I got the flour for the biscuits from the sacks Joe brought up to the house. He said you cut the bags up for dish towels, and bandages." Her eyes went to the scratch on his cheek. "Does your face hurt today?"

"Uh? No, no, my face is fine." That's why it tasted like old jerky, it was old jerky. He hadn't used that saddle bag since spring. Good thing the biscuits had burned. Heaven knows what they would have tasted like; those bags probably had been in the barn for years. He shrugged the shivers off his shoulders. "When you're done eating, I'll give you a more thorough tour, so you know where things are."

"I didn't want to be nosey, poking around your house. I hoped you wouldn't mind that I used the things I did," she said, twisting her spoon around with her fingers.

A smile covered his face. "Well, it's your house too, now, so there's no need to worry about being nosey. Feel free to use whatever you need. And if you don't find something, just ask."

Jessie looked at his full bowl of soup. She couldn't blame him for not liking it. It tasted awful. She was used to eating things that tasted awful, but he probably wasn't.

"I'm afraid I'm not much of a cook. I've never used a stove. Soup is about all I know how to make."

"When I moved out on my own, Stephanie wrote down several recipes so I wouldn't starve. I'll show you were they are, maybe they'll help."

Hope at not being a complete failure as a wife rose in her chest. "Oh, yes, I'm sure I could follow a recipe. Russell was never around much for me to cook for."

Kid leaned forward and pulled something from his back pocket. "I believe this is yours."

Jessie took the hair brush, the only thing she had left from her younger days. She'd gotten it for her fifth birthday. "Yes, it is. Thank you." The tooled silver felt warm and smooth beneath her fingers, reminding her of plaguing thoughts. "Did you go to the soddy today?"

"Yes, I did." He leaned back in his chair and rubbed a hand over his chin.

"Did it survive the storm?" She'd wondered all day about the condition of the little house and worried about who would pick fresh grass for her prairie chickens.

"Not very well."

She sighed. "I was afraid of that. It needs so much work before winter sets in."

"I went there because I thought you might need some of your things. Clothes and such, but I didn't really find much."

She picked the bowls off the table and rose to carry them to the counter. He now knew of her dismal life. He probably thought she was as money hungry and conniving as her brother. "The brush you found is about all I have."

"You don't have any other clothes or-or personal possessions?"

She shook her head. "I had another dress, but had to leave it in Dodge City when we left." After setting the dishes down, she turned to walk back to the table.

Kid stood right behind her and stopped her before she could walk past him. "How long have you been living in the soddy?"

"Almost three months, but I wasn't squatting. I went into Nixon a couple months ago and claimed the land. It's in my name and filed with the government." Her voice trembled. She knew first hand how most people felt about squatters.

"I know you weren't squatting." His hands rubbed her shoulders.

She hadn't felt comforting touches in such a long time. The soothing, warm pressure made her throat burn. Over the years, she'd met many kind people who took sympathy on her situation. Usually, within days if not hours, Russell would do something to make those same people turn their backs on her, simply because she was his sister. The thought made her heart hurt, again, like it had so many times before. That well-known, lonely ache in the middle of her chest also said it would happen again.

She stepped aside and lifted her chin a touch. "No, this time we weren't squatting."

His stare, the one she couldn't see, but felt burning her back as she walked to the table to get the empty bread plate, made her eyes sting.

"What do you mean, this time?" Kid asked.

Jessie twisted to face him. Something in his brown eyes was so kind and caring. She pressed her empty hand against her breastbone, already sorry for whatever the future would bring.

"I've been a squatter before and didn't want to be one again. People are not kind to squatters. People don't like..." her voice trailed away, a thick sob in her throat blocking any other words.

"Aw, sweetheart," he whispered. Solid arms folded her against his chest so tight the plate in her hand flattened between them.

The affectionate, gentle caress of his hands moving across her back and running down the length of her hair offered more compassion than she'd ever known. The sob became uncontrollable and escaped with a croaking sound. Tears began to stream from her eyes. His embrace grew stronger and as soft words of comfort tickled her ears, she wept into his chest. Years of troubling and scaring times floated through her mind.

Jessie cried until she had no tears left, and the sobs eased into slow even breathing. She felt drained and oddly refreshed at the same time. Taking a cleansing breath, she lifted her face from his chest. Gentle brown eyes gazed down, an easy grin lifting the corners of his mouth. The smile made little creases appear in the sun-browned skin around his mouth and eyes.

Her heart somersaulted. The corners of her mouth curved into a smile as she lifted a hand to wipe at the moisture on her cheeks. "I'm sorry, I..."

"Shhh," his lips puckered.

Jessie stared in awe as they lowered to gently brush against her forehead, soft and warm. They floated across her skin, leaving a small trail of healing kisses. She closed her eyes, and a moan released from her throat at the soothing affects.

His lips continued to appease, gliding across her cheeks, touching on her nose. When they touched her mouth, the connection surprised her enough to make her lips part with a slight gasp. The warm sensation flowing through her veins wasn't frightening or upsetting, instead it was encouraging and quite delightful.

Kid's mouth coupled with hers, the movement acted like a leash, pulling her to copy his actions. Their lips joined, then separated and searched for another way to unite, the whole while making the warm stir in her body move faster, until it became heady and desirable. It was so natural, like walking, she didn't need to think as each movement naturally followed another. But Jessie was thinking, thinking kissing Kid was truly amazing and wonderful.

Without lessoning the hold on the plate in her hand, she slipped her arms around his back, wanting more. The solid arms wrapped around her squeezed, pressing oddly sensitive breasts to crush against his firm, molded chest. Enticed, she tilted her head, giving more freedom for their lips to continue. The moan in the back of her throat slipped out as tingles covered every ounce of her frame.

Kid's lips left hers with startling quickness. Jessie blinked in confusion. One hand pressed her face into his shirt front. His chest heaved in and out, matching the movement of hers as his deep voice rumbled above her head, "What Joe?"

From behind a nervous voice answered, "Oh, sorry, I didn't mean to interrupt, I-uh, um..."

Jessie stiffened, but as one of Kid's hands smoothed over her head, she ignored whatever had made her nerves peak and lifted her face to look at him. He stared into her eyes and one of his fingers trailed from her temple to her chin, the soft, silky touch tantalizing. "I'll be right out, Joe," Kid said.

Jessie blinked as his words sunk in, but didn't move. She couldn't, her mind had become fogged over with some kind of a haze.

"All right," Joe mumbled.

The click of the door made something snap and pulled her from the daze. It was like being awakened from a wonderful dream. "I, um..." She swallowed, blinked.

The finger stoking her face moved to cover her lips. "Shh." Kid shook his head. "Shh," he repeated as his lips brushed against her forehead again before he let loose his hold. "I'll go see what he needs, then give you that tour of the house we talked about."

Her cheeks burned and her heart threatened to beat right out of her chest. Neither fear, nor anger, nor any other emotion she could recall had ever made it beat so rapidly. She dared not speak incase it would leap right out her mouth, but Kid stared at her expectantly. So she nodded; a quick, slight, little nod.

He let out a chuckle. It floated in the air like an early bird's song. His fingers lightly pinched her cheek before he turned, walked across the room, and disappeared out the door.

If the table hadn't been right behind her, she may have slipped to the floor. Instead, her melting body leaned against the solid wood. The tin plate in her hand clanged onto the floor. Bewildered, her racing mind wondered how she went from crying in his arms to kissing him, like...like she knew what she was doing. She didn't. She didn't have a clue as to what or how it had happened. Nor how she could make it happen again.

The thought made her eyes widen, and she grabbed the chair for extra support as her knees went weak.

Chapter Six

Kid leaned against the porch rail of the bunkhouse. The boys had delivered each group of cattle: the older ones, in need of grazing to the north pasture, the expecting ones were settled in the south pasture, the young ones further west, and the sickly ones had been brought to the pens near the barn, where he could inspect them and decide exactly what they needed.

Joe had come to tell him they were home, and much to the man's embarrassment, he'd barged in without knocking, which is what he'd always done. Poor Joe was still tongue tied over catching him and Jessie in such an intimate embrace. Kid stood straight and arched his back. Poor Joe, hell…he, Kid Quinter was still coiled tighter than a rattler from the embrace.

A lantern's soft glow flickered from the room he'd settled her in this morning, but no shadows moved about beyond the window. Perhaps she'd fallen asleep with the lamp lit. Kid rocked on the heels of his boots. It had all been so natural. The kiss had just happened. He'd never believed when someone said 'it just happened'. Nothing just happens. There's always cause and affect and people have the ability to control things.

But today- it just happened. One minute he was simply comforting a young, crying girl, and the next he was passionately kissing a young, remarkably beautiful woman- a woman who just happens to be his wife.

"Aw, shit!" Cold coffee spewed out of his mouth, and he dumped the rest onto the ground. Completely unaware he'd even raised the cup to his lips. Setting the empty cup on the rail of the porch he stepped down. The boys had all gone to bed. They were as dog tired as he. A week on the trail, to and from Dodge, and separating the new stock today, had taken all six of the hired hands the Triple Bar employed. His chest puffed with pride of the fact the ranch not only needed the help, but could afford so many ranch hands. Joe had been with him the longest and doubled up as the cook both on the trail and back at the bunk house.

Kid rarely ate with them when they were at the ranch. That wasn't something a cattle baron would do. So he didn't do it. No matter how hungry he was, nor how good the food smelled, he always went to the ranch house and prepared something for himself.

The light still flickered in the second floor bedroom. A shiver raced up his spine as he recalled swallowing the nasty broth. His family may be a little uncouth, but they'd never gone hungry. Something stung in his chest, telling him Jessie had. More than once she'd gone to bed with a very empty tummy. He kicked a rock and continued across the ranch yard. Another hunch said her brother probably always went to bed with a full stomach. Most likely in a warm bed too, nowhere near the soddy Jessie had lived in the past few months.

Kid removed his hat and ran a hand through his hair. There were three things he had to do. One: make sure Jessie had the things she needed, food, shelter, clothes. Two: make sure her brother worked off his debt. And three: make sure a repeat of tonight never happened.

Jessie was nothing more than a scared little girl. It didn't matter how attractive she was, whether she could read and write, or even cook, she could never become the woman he needed as a wife. He was a cattle baron and cattle barons only married exotic women from Europe.

He replaced his hat and opening the back door of the house, gave a sharp whistle. "Sammy! Here boy!" He waited, listening for the sound of paws tearing across grass and gravel. Nothing but silence filled his ears.

"Fine, stay out, I'm too tired to wait for you." Still frustrated with his lack of control, he shut the door behind him with more force than necessary. He took a deep breath and shook the tension from his body like a horse quivering off flies. Walking across the room, he turned down the wicks of the oil lamps as he made his way through the house, toward his bedroom.

At the top of the stairs a door loomed before him. Was she sleeping? Should he check? Maybe turn out the light shining beneath the door? As the cold steel of the knob filled his palm a low growl came from inside the room. His hand tightened its grasp, slowly twisting the doorknob. The growl grew louder and more menacing.

Damn dog! Kid knelt down near the key hole and whispered, "Sammy! Shush!"

The growl came again.

"Damn it, Sammy, you're gonna wake her." The words had no sooner left his mouth when the door opened. Tiny, bare toes stuck out from beneath the frayed hem of her faded dress. His face grew warm as his gaze followed the flow of material upwards where it connected with light blue eyes. "I uh- I was- Sammy," he stammered.

"He doesn't seem to want to leave my side. I'm sorry I shouldn't have shut the door," Jessie said.

Did she think he'd been peeking through the key hole of her door? More embarrassed than he recalled being in a very long time, Kid stood and locked shaking knees. He rubbed the back of his neck and looked somewhere over her shoulder. Anywhere but into her appealing, little face.

"No, no that's fine. You can shut the door. He can sleep in there. I just, uh, didn't know where he was."

On cue, Sammy stepped in front of her and lifted his head. The lab looked him up and down, almost as if questioning Kid's presence. Who the hell did the dog think he was?

As if Sammy had read his mind, the dog sat on his haunches, narrowed his eyes, and lifted the corners of his mouth to show large, canine teeth.

Kid curled his lip, warningly staring back at the dog. Sammy glanced up at Jessie with puppy-love eyes. Her hand came down to pat him on the head. Kid could have sworn the dog smiled at her before turning to glare at him again.

"I'm going to bed. I'll see you both in the morning." First his body betrayed him, then his dog. He felt like stomping a foot. The thought shocked him. He was becoming one of his brothers. He let out a deep, heavy sigh and turned to walk down the hall.

"Kid, er, Mr. Quinter?"

He pivoted. Sammy followed her into the hall.

"Um, did you still want to show me the pantry and root cellar?" Her soft voice floated through the air like a faraway songbird.

"No, we can do it tomorrow. Or you can just look around." He didn't have the willpower to be that close to her again tonight. Swiftly, he turned and began to walk toward his room. "You'll eventually find everything."

"Oh, well then, good-night," she whispered.

Something made him stop and turn around

again. The moonlight shining in through the hall window, along with the glow of the lamp from her room, basked her form with a faint golden halo. She resembled what he'd expect a hallucination to look like; a pure, simple vision of loveliness. Kid gave his head a quick shake, but the image didn't change.

"Good night, Jessie." He bolted for the solitude of his room.

****

Ahead, a lopsided wagon rolled down the road. Kid reined Jack to a stop and waited for it to approach. The wheels came to a halt with a loud clunk. "You have a hub out of round, Hog," he said.

"Yeah, I know. That new handyman you hired fixed it this morning," Hog grunted.

"What new handyman?"

Bug's face lit up. "Russ, your wife's brother. He decided he'd start working off his debt right away, so he's been doing odd jobs around the house."

Kid frowned. "That's not the deal I made with him."

"Yeah, but Sheriff Turley said he shouldn't go over to your house until next week. And Kid, you're not gonna believe it, but he's found so much work around our place, he almost has your bill paid off. Ma's keeping track," Bug said.

Irritation made his nostrils flair. He tightened his hold on Jack's reins. The horse tossed his head and took a step sideways. He relaxed his fingers and gave Jack's neck a calming pat.

"The work he's doing for Ma will have to pay for his board and room there. He'll work at my place to pay off what he owes for Miss Molly." He knew the guy was going to try and get out of the deal, but he hadn't thought it would be this quick.

"You'll have to take that up with Ma," Hog shot him a weary look.

Kid raised an eyebrow. Hog never said a lot, but

his facial expressions did. And the one he gave right now clearly said Russell Johnson was more work than he was worth.

"I will. You two turn that wagon around and take it slow back to the house. I'll help you fix it before I leave."

"You coming over for a visit? You ain't still sore at us, are ya, Kid?" Hope filled Bug's young eyes.

Hog, only a year older than Bug, gave a hopeful glance his way as well.

Kid smiled. "Yeah, I'm coming over to visit, and I'm not sore at either of you. I'll meet you at the house." He gave a wave and nudged Jack into a canter. He'd bet his bottom dollar Russell Johnson was making plans to be long gone by the time next week rolled around.

Jack made the ride a quick one, and interestingly enough, Russell Johnson was saddling one of the horses Kid had loaned his family.

"Going somewhere?" Kid brought Jack to a halt in the doorway of the barn.

Russell stepped away from the gelding. His eyes shifted around before he said, "Your mother needs some supplies from town. I'm going to go get them."

"Why didn't she ask Bug and Hog to pick them up with the wagon?" Kid dismounted.

"They had already left when she remembered a couple other things." Russell sidestepped, moving closer to a bulky flour sack on the barn floor.

He pretended not to notice and rested an arm on the top rail of a stall. "Where are Skeeter and Snake?"

"They left early this morning. I don't know where they went. I better get to town. Your Ma will tan my hide if I don't get back with those supplies real quick," Russell said, but didn't move back toward the horse.

"No, I don't think you'll be going anywhere,

Russ." Kid added the name for insult. "Pull the saddle off that horse."

"Go ask your Ma, if you don't believe me."

"We'll go ask her together. Right after you pull that saddle down and put the horse away." He could hold his temper, had years of practice with his brothers, but Russell Johnson pushed it. "Now!"

Russell puckered his lips like a five year old and shuffled toward the horse. He flipped the saddle off the gelding and set it on the saddle rack. The whole time sending pouting stares at Kid.

"Lead the gelding to the corral out back," Kid said.

Russell's eyes went from the bag near his feet to the back door. "No, I'll just put him in a stall for now."

"No, you'll put him in the corral like I told you." Kid let his eyes rest on the bag for a few seconds before he added, "Now, Russ."

Russell started to bend down for the bag. Kid shot forward and snatched it from his reach.

"That's mine!" Russell tried to catch the end of the bag.

"I really doubt it." Kid set the bag near his feet. "Take the gelding to the corral."

Russell stomped his foot, and with more force than necessary, yanked on the reins in his hand. The gelding reacted by tossing his head aside. Russell pulled harder which only irritated the horse more.

Kid watched the tug of war, knowing the horse would win, and the man would get what he deserved. It happened a few moments later. The gelding rose up and his front hooves pawed at the air. Russell yelped and stumbled backwards. His feet slipped in a pile of horse debris and over he went. A loud crack echoed as the back of his head hit the top rung of a stall gate. The gelding shot forward, barely missing the sprawled form.

The man moaned loud enough to be heard in Texas. Feeling no compassion, Kid kicked one of the shiny boots.

"Go get the bridle off that horse. He's gonna trip on the reins."

"I can't, I think I'm bleeding," Russell groaned.

"Not yet, but you will be if that horse breaks a leg. Now get up."

"You go get it. Damn horse is wild as hell. I'm not going near him. I'm injured."

"Like hell you're injured." He grabbed the front of Russell's suit jacket and lifted until the man's toes barely touched the ground. Glaring deep into pale blue eyes, he seethed, "Get the bridle before I injure you. Believe me- you'll know you're injured then." With a hard shove, he thrust Russell toward the back of the barn.

The man stumbled forward, trying to catch his footing. Between the slime on his boots and the hay on the ground, Russell didn't gain control of his feet until he ran into the back wall. This time the front of his head smacked the wood.

If he hadn't felt so pissed off, he might have laughed at the sight. He glared at the man, matching the hateful stare Russell shot over his shoulder before stumbling to the door.

Keeping an eye on him, Kid reached down and picked up the sack before he followed. The gelding played his part well, and a smiled tugged at Kid's lips before Russell finally got the bridle off the horse and stepped around the larger piles of dung on his way back to the barn.

Kid waited until Russell was almost to the barn before he tipped the bag and let the sun bleached bones fall onto the ground.

"What the hell are you doing?" Russell increased his speed, trying to stop the bones from falling in the muck.

"What's so special about a few old bones?" he asked.

"They're not just old bones." Russell tossed the bridle into the barn and reached down to gather the bones. "These are buffalo bones."

"Yeah, I know what kind of bones they are."

"They're a precious commodity. They get shipped east where they make china out of them." Russell grabbed the sack from the ground and began to set the bones in the bag with care.

Kid leaned against the barn door. His gaze went from the bridle, which he'd paid a fair amount for, to the useless bones. "So you plan on taking them to Dodge to be shipped east?"

"If you must know, yes I am. I plan on giving the money to your family." Russell held the sack up in front of him. "This little bag is easily worth the fifty bucks you claim I owe them."

Kid snorted, seriously trying to hold in a chuckle. "Not hardly."

"Buffalo bones are bringing six to eight dollars a pound right now," Russell said.

"Who told you that?"

"I saw the sign in Dodge."

"I think you misread a very old sign. The bones used to bring six to eight dollars a *ton*. But the Buffalo have been gone for over five years. The only bones being found now aren't good for anything more than fertilizer," Kid explained.

"A ton?"

"Yes, a ton. Those few bones are worth less than the bag you've got them in."

"Shit!" Russell threw the bag on the ground.

"Pick it up. And the bridle." The rattle of a wagon pulling in the yard echoed into the barn, making Kid add, "You've a wagon hub to repair."

Russell grabbed the bag and walked over to retrieve the bridle. "What are they doing back already?"

"It seems your hub job didn't hold. Pull it apart. I'll show you the correct way to fix it when I'm done talking with Ma." Halfway to the barn door, Kid stopped to ask, "Where are Skeeter and Snake?"

"Out gathering buffalo bones," Russell mumbled.

Shaking his head, he walked out of the barn. They should have known those bones were useless. When would his brothers grow up? Snake was over eighteen now, and Skeeter pushing twenty-one. He waved at Hog, motioning to pull the wagon up next to the barn while making his way to the house. At least the entertaining show had eased his anger, he actually let out a laugh as he hopped up the steps.

****

Jessie pulled the golden brown loaf of bread from the oven. It smelled heavenly. The directions she'd found of Stephanie's were easy to follow, and the unending supplies she'd discovered in the pantry and cellar made her feel like Christmas time when mama and papa were alive. A cherry pie sat on the counter, ready to go in the oven as soon as she put the bread on a cloth to cool.

The loaf grew hot in her hands. Used pots, pans, bowls and spoons filled every flat surface. She set the bread pan on top of the stove and went to clear an area on the table.

Sammy's bark startled her before the spot was clear.

"Sammy!" She turned to where he sat in front of the stove. The dog looked at her and barked again before looking at the stovetop.

"Oh, no!" she exclaimed.

The items in her hands scattered onto the floor as she scurried across the room to where smoke billowed from beneath the bottom of the bread pan. She'd accidentally set the bread pan on top of the towel she'd used to protect her hands from the hot metal, which she'd set on top of a hot burner.

Using the skirt of her dress to prevent a burn, she grabbed the bread pan with one hand and pushed the smoking towel to the floor with the other. Heat already burning her skin through the thin material of her dress, she rushed to set the hot pan on the table.

Sammy barked again.

"Now what?" Jessie turned in time to see flames rise from the towel on the floor.

"Oh, no!" She leaped forward, frantically stomping on the flaming towel.

Thankfully, it was several hours before Sammy barked again, this time because Kid had rode into the yard. Jessie squared her shoulders and took a deep breath. Everything was in its proper place. The food was done, the table set, and she hoped all of the burnt smells had cleared from the air. A quiver touched her spine. The only thing she hadn't been able to repair was the small burn mark in the middle of the kitchen floor. Scouring hadn't helped, the wood had been charred.

She pressed a hand to the guilt racing across her chest. Hopefully Kid wouldn't notice. She smoothed the hair out of her eyes, took another deep breath, and waited for the back door to open. At the last moment, she scurried over to stand on the black spot, waving for Sammy to come and sit next to her feet.

Before the door opened all the way, she blurted, "Hi. How was your day?"

Kid stepped into the room. His eyes grew wide as they settled on her face. His brows drew together, making lines crease the area between them.

"Hello," he said before he looked around the room.

Jessie pointed to the table. "I found Stephanie's recipes and all of the supplies. I promise tonight's meal is much better than last night's."

Kid's eyes stopped on her again. They went from her head to her toes and back up again. "You've been cooking?" His face formed a grimace.

She nodded, trying to hold in her smile.

Sammy barked.

"He helped." She pointed to the dog by her knee.

"I see."

"Sit down. It's all ready."

"Jessie, uh…"

"Honest, I sampled it. It's good," she said. Worry made her voice quiver slightly. To her it tasted fine, but then again, she was use to flavorless food.

A smile formed on his face. "I'm sure it is." Kid shook his head as he walked to the table.

Jessie leaned down and whispered in Sammy's ear, "Please lay right here on this burn spot. I don't want him to see it until after he eats."

Sammy let out a little moan, but did lie down. Using his hind legs, the dog spun his prone body around so he faced the table, then settled his head atop his paws.

Kid looked from the dog to her. He let out a soft chuckle as his gaze went between them again. Jessie noticed a long white streak running along the dog's back. She rubbed at the area with her hand. "I must have spilt a touch of flour on him today."

"Just a touch maybe." Kid let out another chuckle as he shook his head again.

Jessie settled into her chair at the table. "I made a beef roast with potatoes and carrots, bread, and a cherry pie for dessert." Her cheeks burned at how boastful she sounded, but she couldn't control the pride coming out as she pointed to each dish on the table. "Go ahead, try some."

Kid reached over and picked up her plate. "Ladies first," he said as he removed the lid from the pan in the middle of the table and began to scoop contents onto her plate.

He sniffed the air above her plate before he set it in front of her and picked up his. She sliced the bread and handed him a piece. "I didn't know we had a milk cow either. Joe showed me where the butter churn was." Her head nodded toward the bowl of smooth butter.

"He did, did he?"

"Yes, and he showed me the ice box, and explained how it works. He said he'd teach me to milk the cow another day. He was already done with the milking when he came in this morning." She stopped talking as he lifted a forkful of food to his mouth and held her breath as he chewed then swallowed.

His eyes met hers. "This is very good, Jessie." He nodded and filled his fork again. "Very good."

"Thank you." Tickled, she couldn't help but send a wide smile to Sammy. The dog lifted his head and gave a soft bark.

Chapter Seven

Kid fought to pull his eyes from the delightful girl sitting across from him. Sammy didn't look nearly as disheveled as she did. Flour covered her body from head to toe, every time she moved a puff of white came from somewhere. A glob of bread dough, pie crust, or perhaps butter, smeared one cheek, while a long, black streak stretched down the other. All of it made her look more adorable than anything he'd ever seen.

Her hard work had paid off. The meal was delicious. At least what he'd tasted so far and the pie sitting beside his plate looked close to perfect. The neat and clean kitchen might have made him wonder if she'd conjured up the meal if she didn't look like she'd just fought a war with a flour tornado.

"I'm sorry I wasn't up when you left this morning. I didn't realize you got up so early. I'll be up tomorrow to make you breakfast." Her soft voice broke his thoughts.

Kid resumed eating, savoring each mouthful. "That's not necessary. I can manage my own breakfast. Besides, I won't have to leave as early tomorrow."

"Where did you have to go today?" she asked.

"I rode over to my mother's."

The fork stalled near her mouth. "Oh, how are your mother and brothers?"

"Good, I helped the boys fix a hub on one of the wagons." He took a second helping of roast and potatoes.

"That was nice of you."

She chewed her food very slowly. The way her brows pulled together as she stared at her plate made Kid wonder if thoughts of her brother filled her head. He'd have to bring up the subject. He lifted his fork and determined it could wait until after they ate. "Stephanie sent some things home for you."

"She did?" Her gaze lifted, clearly confused. "What sort of things?"

"They're out on the back porch. I'll carry them in when we're done. It's just some things that no longer fit her. She thought they might fit you."

"Clothes?" Her eyes sparkled. "Did she say if it's a dress? Or maybe a nightgown?" She was almost breathless.

He smiled, but warned, "Don't get too excited, they may not fit. She said she'd come over and show you how to alter them if you'd like."

"Really? Oh, that is so kind of her." Her smile was brighter than any morning sunrise he'd ever seen.

Kid chuckled. "Night before last she held you at gun point. I wouldn't think you'd think she was kind after that."

"That was circumstantial." She shook her head. "You mustn't hold it against her."

He closed his gapping mouth. She really was quite unbelievable. A silly, happy feeling settle in his chest as he picked up his knife and asked, "Are you ready for a piece of this pie that looks good enough to eat?"

She scooped the last morsels on her plate onto her fork. "Yes, I think I am."

The pie was as good as it looked. Kid had two pieces, making sure the first one hadn't just been teasing his taste buds. When they finished, she rose to clear the table. He patted his stomach. "You out did yourself, Jessie. Thank you, it really was delicious."

"You're welcome." She lifted the dishes from the table. "I have to admit, I was quite nervous when I started this morning. And I discovered I'm not a very neat cook."

"Oh?" He rose to help carry items from the table.

"Yes, had you come home this afternoon, I would have been embarrassed for you to see the mess I'd made." A cloud of white hung in her wake.

"Hmmm," he said, holding a chuckle. His foot bumped something, making him stumble. He caught his faltered steps and pulled his gaze from her cloudy trail to glance to the floor. "Sammy, move out of the way."

"No!" Dishes clattered into the sink before she rushed to the dog. "No, I promised he could lie there for being such a good dog today." She knelt to pat the wide, black head. Her nervous glance bounced between him and Sammy. "Didn't I boy?"

Sammy's tail thumped the floor. Kid frowned.

She twisted, reaching for the dishes he held. "Here, I'll take those."

As she stood her skirt flared, showing the frayed hem was streaked with black soot. Kid took a second look. Several long brown scorch marks trailed up the front of the material. "Jessie, did you have trouble starting a fire in the stove today?"

"Huh? Starting a fire? No, no, I didn't have any problems starting a fire today." She set the dishes down on the counter, shaking her head.

Kid stepped forward to get a closer look. His foot stumbled against the dog again. "Damn it, Sammy, move!"

The dog yelped and jumped to scramble out of his way, leaving a large black spot on the floor.

Thinking it was mud from the dog, Kid ran the toe of his boot over the area.

"Kid, uh, Mr. Quinter, I'm so terribly sorry. It really was an accident." Jessie's face became distorted. It made her look even more adorable. She lifted her hands, hiding the view from him.

"An accident?" he asked, taking a quick glance around the room.

She lowered her hands, wrung them together, and stared at the spot below his boot.

He slipped his foot aside, taking a closer look at the darkened area. Recognition followed closely by concern made his throat tighten. His gaze went to the scorch marks on her dress.

"Jesus! Did you catch yourself on fire? Are you burnt?" Heart pounding, he leaped forward, landing on his knees. Without thought to impropriety, he lifted her dress to check her legs for burns.

"Should I get the balm?" Flipping the material over his shoulder, his hands moved over the white, smooth skin, searching for red blisters or welts.

The back door flew open, hitting the wall with a smack. "Hey boss, we gotta talk about this new fella you brought home."

Kid turned to the sound, one hand fought to push frayed material out of his eyes. Flour dust puffed from the fabric as he batted it aside. When it settled, draping his head and shoulders, he stared up at Joe.

"Oh, uh, sorry!" Joe turned beet red and shot back out the door.

Blood rushed to his cheeks, burning and tingling. Had he just been caught with his head under her skirt? Something under his fingers trembled, making him realize one hand was still wrapped around her leg. All of a sudden his fingers felt like they were on fire.

Blowing out a gust of air, Kid pulled his fingers

from her shin and backed out from beneath her skirt. "You, um." He paused, cleared his throat. "You didn't get burnt?" It hadn't helped, he sounded like a croaking frog.

"No, no, I didn't."

Frozen- like a petrified rock- he stayed there, on his hands and knees, staring at the varnished wood floor. After the universe had tick-tocked what felt like an hour, but most likely was less than a minute, he stood and taking the chance his weather-beaten face wouldn't show his embarrassment, looked at her.

"What happened?"

"I accidentally set a towel on top of the stove and when I pushed it off, the air made it catch afire. My dress got scorched while I was stomping it out. I'm so sorry I burned your floor. I scrubbed it, but I'm afraid the wood is scorched." Both hands were pressed against her chest and with eyes as sad as a hound dog, she faced him. Her whole body shivered like leaves in the wind.

He stepped forward, cradled the soft skin of her cheeks with his palms. Cheerless blue eyes tugged at his heart. "Don't worry about the floor, sweetheart. All that matters is you weren't hurt."

"I wasn't." Her head gave a sad little shake.

It was so easy to care about her, so easy to want to comfort her. He pulled her forward and slipped his arms around her trembling frame. With a mind of their own, his lips lowered to kiss the top of her head. A puff of flour almost made him sneeze. "You've had quite a day."

Her head nodded against his chest.

He tightened his hold, wanting to absorb the quakes. Slowly her shivers eased and soft curves settled against him. "Would you like me to help you clean up the kitchen?" he asked.

"No, I can do it."

A sharp pain made him pull his teeth off his bottom lip, which he'd unknowingly bit while trying to hold off the new urges taking over his body. The cool night air would do him some good.

"I'm going to go see what Joe needs, and then I'll carry those clothes in for you." The need was so strong he had to place one more kiss on her hair before he released her.

Jessie stepped back, lifting apologetic eyes. She ran both hands over her face, which caused the globs to smear further across her delicate skin. "Thank you," she murmured.

Kid lifted a cloth off the counter and wiped the smudges from both of her cheeks. "You're welcome." He fought the need to kiss her again. A real, solid kiss like last night. He set the cloth down and turned for the door. His cheeks once again grew warm at the thought of facing Joe after the unusual position the man had caught him in. *Damn.* He hadn't been embarrassed for years. Now it had happened two days in a row.

"Kid?" Her voice stopped him as he grasped the door handle.

The way she said his name, soft and sweet sounding, made his knees weak. "Yes?" he croaked.

"Who's the new fellow Joe needs to talk to you about?"

He took a deep breath. His cheeks puffed as he blew it out, not wanting to answer, but knowing he had to, he said, "Your brother."

A deep frown covered her face. "R-Russell's here?"

He nodded. "I brought him home with me."

One tiny hand stretched forward as she stepped toward him. Something close to fear filled her eyes. "Can, can I just say in advance, I'm sorry? For whatever he may do, I'm sorry. Please know I don't have control over what he does. I-I…"

He took the out-stretched hand. Clammy and cold, the fingers shook beneath his.

"Jessie, I won't ever hold you accountable for someone else's actions." He ran his fingers over the thin digits. "Anything Russell does, Russell will have to correct. Not you. I promise, you won't have to pay for his dealings ever again." He carried the fingers to his lips and kissed the back of her hand. "Trust me."

She gave a slight nod.

"Good, now do up the dishes. I'll be back with the trunks in a few minutes."

"Trunks?"

Happy to see the shine come back into her eyes, he nodded. "Yes, Stephanie sent two trunks full of clothes for you to go through."

"Two trunks full?" A wide smile covered her face.

His heart skipped a beat. "Yes, sweetheart, two trunks full." He gave her hand a final squeeze before he released it and walked out the door.

As the door clicked shut, Jessie's shoulders slumped. A solid lump formed in the pit of her stomach. Russell was here. Today had been the best day of her life, mostly because not once had she worried about what Russell was up to, and how it would cause havoc.

Sammy brushed against her leg and lifted his head, big brown eyes asking what was wrong.

"It's not that I don't love my brother, I do. I just don't like how he refuses to work, to do anything constructive and long term. All he ever focuses on are ways to make money so he can live the good life. It's all he talks about." She ran a hand over his wide head, happy she had someone to talk to. The dog had become her friend, the best one she'd ever had.

"Oh, Sammy, he's bound to mess things up again." Frustrated, Jessie slapped at her thighs. A puff of flour rose to float around her legs.

"Goodness!"

The washroom off the kitchen stood before her. A room she had yet to venture into. For some reason it seemed too intimate of an area.

"Would Kid mind if I used it?" she asked the dog.

Sammy padded across the floor, stopped near the door and barked. Her feet moved toward the room, and her fingers plucked at the front of the dress. A new white cloud puffed with each flick. She must look a mess.

The door swung open, and she made her way into the small room. A reflection in the mirror instantly caught her attention. A gasp escaped her lips. Not only was her dress full of flour, but her hair looked gray from the white stuff. She turned to Sammy.

"Why didn't you tell me I'm covered in flour?" Her eyes fluttered shut as she recalled carrying the heavy bag from the pantry to the table. It weighed a ton, and an explosion of white had filled the room when she hefted it onto the table.

Sammy barked again. She peeked at him through her fingers. One paw sat on the rim of the large tub. How long had it been since she'd taken a bath in a tub? Not since she was fourteen or so and they'd stayed a winter with a widow near Topeka. She'd been a kind woman, but after she caught Russell stealing from her jewelry box, they had to leave. A shiver ran up her spine- it had been a cold and rainy night. One that made her think they'd freeze to death before the light of morning came.

She ran a hand along the rim. Since then she'd bathed in streams and rivers, even at the soddy all she had were small buckets. This tub's basin was deep, and the brass smooth to the touch. It would be easy to wash her hair with all this room. She pushed a long lock of the mass behind one ear. Kid had said

Stephanie sent two trunks of clothes. If only there would be a night gown amongst the woman's castaways. It had been years since she'd had sleeping clothes.

A wide smile covered her face, and she reached down to hug Sammy before flipping around to scurry from the room to clean up the kitchen and heat water. The thought of feeling fresh and clean and slipping into new clothes filled her with a sense of joy she hadn't experienced in a very long time.

All day, thoughts and activities had filled her with excitement and delight. Feelings she'd forgotten existed. She squeezed the water from the rag in the dish pan and moved to the table to wipe away a few bread crumbs. Her hand stilled midway across the table. Russell was here now. He'd find a way to shatter those feelings. Always did.

The rag began to move again with new determination. *No, not this time!* Kid had said people always had a choice, and that meant her too. She could choose not to let Russell's actions thwart her life. It was time for her to start making her own choices and living her own life.

After a final swipe, she tossed the rag at the dish tub and walked to the stove. Setting the largest pot atop the burner, she stoked the fire then filled the kettle with water. With a bucket in hand, she moved to the back door. It would take a lot of water to fill the bathing tub, and she was going to enjoy each and every drop. Jessie patted her leg, encouraging Sammy to rise and follow her out the door.

****

Jessie carried bucket after bucket of water into the house. Kid's first reaction had been to look at the widows to see if flames licked at the glass panes. Concluding she must be filling the large, brass tub in the washroom, he tried to hurry the conversation with Joe, but the man was fit to be tied over Russell Johnson. The arrogant little ass had attempted to claim Joe's single room on the far side of the bunk house. Declaring the ranch owner's wife's brother deserved the privacy instead of sharing one of the bunk beds with the other hands.

Kid refused to step in. Instead, he told Joe it was up to him to set the rules for Russell just as he did with all the new hands. Russell was no exception, and he wasn't going to let the man believe he was by stepping in to settle this first dispute.

"But Kid, I don't want Jessie thinking I'm a bad guy," Joe said as they leaned against the hitching post outside the bunkhouse.

"A bad guy?" When Jessie entered the back door, he turned to look at the man.

"Yeah, a bad guy. She's a sweet little thing."

Kid frowned. "You just met her."

"Yeah, well I just met her brother too. I have a hard time believing they're kin. My first impressions are always right."

"Really?" Kid shuffled his feet. It felt like there was a little worm wiggling around in his stomach.

"Yeah, like that hand you wanted to hire in Dodge last year. I told you no, he wouldn't work out, but you hired him anyway, and sure enough, he didn't work out."

"What about the several you've hired over the years? The ones that haven't worked out?" Kid straightened his stance, glancing back to the sound of a door opening. She walked back out of the house, carrying two buckets. He needed to go help her. Pretty soon she'd be too worn out to enjoy her bath.

"Would you just tell him he stays where I put him?" Joe said.

Tired of the conversation, he said, "Nope. You're the foreman. You handle the men, I handle the business. But before you go in, come help me carry those trunks, I had the boys unload, up to her room." Kid started walking toward the house, knowing the man would follow. Just as he knew Joe could handle Russell Johnson. Besides, his mind was too busy hoping the clothes Stephanie sent would fit Jessie. She was so excited about the garments, he really didn't want to see her disappointed.

They lugged the trunk through the back door. Every kettle he owned sat on the stove, steam rose from a couple of them and water sloshed into the brass tub in the washroom. He pulled on the handle of the trunk, making Joe walk faster as he carried the other end. He forced the man to hurry through the kitchen and up the stairs.

"Hey slow down." Joe stumbled on yet another step. "What you got in this thing? Rocks?"

"No, they're Jessie's things."

"Oh, well then, slow down, we don't want to break anything."

Over his shoulder, he shot the man a questioning look. The little worm in his stomach began to crawl around again. He slowed his feet, not really knowing if it was for Joe's sake or if it was to examine the little worm.

He lowered his end of the trunk near the foot of her bed. In all the years he'd known Joe, the man had never been overly concerned about anyone but himself. But here he was in a fret over Jessie, her brother, her belongings. A scowl pulled on his forehead.

Joe stopped in the doorway. "Are you coming? Ain't that other one hers too?"

"Yeah, it's hers," he snapped.

Joe met his gaze. "What?"

"What-what?"

"What you thinking so hard about? You look like you just ate something sour."

"Must be the company." Kid walked past him

and started down the stairs.

"I ain't done nothin' for you to be grumpy about."

"Nothing but barge in the house every night," he tossed over his shoulder.

"I said I was sorry 'bout that. I'll start knocking."

"Yeah, well you better." Kid stopped in the doorway to the kitchen, scanning the area. He sure didn't want Joe to see Jessie if she was already starting to undress. The little worm wiggled faster. He'd also have to see about getting some curtains to cover the windows in the wash room. Any one of the boys could walk by and see in.

Joe brushed past him. "What did you say you were doin'? Checking her legs for burns?" An amused laugh floated in the air as the man walked across the kitchen.

Kid stomped out the door behind him. He couldn't be jealous, he'd never been jealous of anyone in his life. He respected people, set goals to achieve the things he wanted, but he'd never been jealous. The thought was extremely irritating- almost as irritating as Joe.

Kid pointed across the yard and said, "Go to the bunkhouse. I got this one myself."

Joe reached down and grabbed a handle on the far end of the trunk. "This one looks heavier than the last. I'll help you."

He grasped the handle and pulled the trunk toward him. "I gotta it."

Joe hefted his end into the air. "I'll help."

Kid gave it a hard tug. "I said I got it."

Joe tugged his way. "And I said I'd help."

Jessie paused on the top step of the back porch. She'd made a dozen trips to the well, and needed a moment to catch her breath.

"Do you need help?" she asked the two men tugging on the large trunk.

Joe dropped his end. It hit the porch floor with a loud thud. His hands stretched toward her water bucket.

"Here, Miss, I'll get that for you."

Kid stepped in front of the man and pulled the handle from her hand before Joe could grasp it.

"I'll get that for you, Jessie." He turned to Joe. "It is Missus not Miss."

"Well then why don't you show the Missus how to use the pump in the house so she doesn't need to lug water in?" Joe asked. One side of his lip was curled up. It reminded her of Sammy when he was irritated.

Noticing Kid's face, she took a step sideways. Air locked in her lungs at the way he glared at Joe. She grasped the hand rail to keep her balance.

Kid glanced at her before looking back to the man. "Go to bed, Joe."

Joe pushed his way past Kid and down the steps. "Yeah, I think I will." Walking past her, he tipped the edge of his hat. "Good night, Mrs. Quinter."

Jessie tried to talk but only a slight whisper emitted, "Good night, Joe."

"Where did you want this?" Kid asked.

Without meeting his eyes, she glanced to the bucket he held. "I-I can take it."

"No, I've got it. In the washroom or the kitchen?" His tone was kind, not the harsh one he'd used with Joe.

She snuck a peek. His eyes no longer looked like they were full of fire. Realizing she still held her breath, she let it seep out and said, "The kitchen, it's for morning."

He stepped aside and waved his empty hand for her to enter. She hoped her trembling toes wouldn't trip and moved forward. Kid carried the bucket over near the stove. Sammy went to sniff at it as he set the pail down on the small stool which acted as a base for it. She'd learned earlier Sammy thought it was his personal drinking container if you set it on the floor.

"Do you know how to prime a pump?" Kid asked.

Bringing her mind away from the dog, she shook her head negatively.

"The house is built over White Woman Creek," he said as he walked to the counter by the sink. "The creek starts in Colorado, but a few miles west of here it drains into the White Woman Basin, and from there it flows underground to the Arkansas River." Carrying a small pitcher, he went back to the water bucket. "That's why you had such a good well at your soddy." He filled the pitcher and went back to the sink.

"I tried to use that pump, but nothing came out," she said.

"There's a leather gasket in it. If it dries out, it won't pump. It probably dried out while I was on the drive. I'm sorry for not thinking to prime it for you. Come here." He waved an arm for her to step closer.

She did and watched as he poured the water from the pitcher into the spout. He began to pump the handle with quick even strokes. His was so big and brawny. The muscles in his arm bulged with each movement.

"Once the leather gets wet again it'll swell and form a suction to pull the water up out of the ground."

Hoping he didn't notice the way her eyes ogled, she turned to the gurgling noises sounding from the pump. After a few more thrusts, water began to flow out of the squared spout. Jessie grabbed the large bowl she used to wash dishes in and set it below the streaming water. Kid gave her a quizzical look.

"Jessie, do you know this wash tub has a drain?"

"A what?" she asked, while silently wondering

why her mind became fuzzy whenever he stood beside her.

He lifted the bowl and tipped the water out of it. Jessie watched as it flowed down a hole in the bottom. Kid stepped back and opened the wide door below the sink. He pointed. "That is a drain pipe. I read all I could about indoor plumbing before I built the house. The water runs through this pipe under the floor, it meets up with the water from the tub in the wash room and then drains into a pit out back."

"It does?" He had to be the smartest man she'd ever met.

"Yes, all the major cities have indoor plumbing any more. I plan on putting in an indoor toilet as soon as they perfect them. From what I've read, they produce gas that can be harmful, and they haven't mastered an exhaust system yet."

Jessie cheeks burned as he spoke of such private matters.

He chuckled. "There's nothing to be embarrassed about." He patted the sink. "This tub is made of soapstone. I had it shipped in from New Hampshire. It's guaranteed to never leak, crack, or decay. It's virtually indestructible."

She leaned forward and touched the hard surface. It wasn't like any she'd ever seen before, but most of the house was like nothing she'd ever seen before.

"I built the cabinet around it after it arrived. The catalog showed it standing alone, but I liked this idea. I saw it in another book."

"You did a fine job." She looked around. "You built this whole house by yourself?"

"Most of it. The boys helped me with some things." Kid picked up a small, round disk. "This is the plug. When you want it to hold water just push this in the hole."

"I found one like that for the tub in the wash

room." She let out a small laugh. "After my first two buckets of water disappeared."

He joined her laughter. When it died down, he glanced around. "Well, I'll carry in your other trunk."

"I'll help," she offered, not quite ready to be separated from him.

"I got it. I put the other one up in your room if you want to go see what's in it." He glanced down at her flour covered dress. The wide smile on his face made her heart skip a beat.

"You did?" The thought of a new dress was extremely compelling, almost as delightful sounding as a bath, but neither of those could be as pleasurable as standing next to him. A blush made her cheeks grow warm. She glanced around, her gaze landed on the stove. Little spirals of steam rose from the smaller two kettles. She stuck her finger into one of the larger ones. "The water isn't hot yet," she surmised aloud.

"Then go look at your new clothes. I'll carry the other trunk up to you."

"Thank you." She scurried from the room to take the stairs two at a time. It had been so long since she had something new to wear. Before mama and papa died she'd had several dresses, but…

"No," she said aloud. "I'm no longer going to think of the past, only the future, and how I can make it better." All of the things Kid had accomplished made her believe she too could have a much better life than what she'd had the past few years. He had to be the smartest man on earth, and probably the kindest. She paused at the top of the stairs, her heart skipping every other beat. Was *he* really *her* husband?

She entered her room. The trunk sat at the foot of the big bed. Smooth, shiny wood sparkled as moonlight streaming in the window bounced off the round top. She lit the lamp on the table beside the bed and turned the wick as high as it could safely go. She hurried back to the trunk and sat down on the floor in front of it. Her fingers ran across the wood before grasping the brass catch. Her mind swirled like a Kansas dust devil. It all seemed impossible. Overnight she'd gone from a leaking sod house, scraping everyday to find food to eat, with no hope of things changing, to living in a mansion, having a pantry and root cellar full of food, and married to the nicest, most handsome man on earth.

Her fingers stalled. Married? She didn't feel married. But then again, she really didn't know what being married should feel like. She shrugged her shoulders. How did someone learn how to become a wife?

Sammy, never far from her side, bumped her arm with his wet nose. She smiled. "You're right." After rubbing his soft fur, she turned back to the trunk. "We'll worry about that later. Right now it's time to see what's in this trunk."

She twisted and tugged, but no matter what she tried, the latch wouldn't let loose. The front clasp flipped up and down beneath her fingers, but something still held it shut. Her nose pressed against the side of the box as she tried to see between the thin openings, hoping to figure out how the contraption worked.

A thud startled her. She glanced up. The second box sat on the floor behind her. Kid put both hands on his knees and knelt forward, taking a couple deep breaths.

"Thank you," she said before her gaze went back to the trunk.

"Need some help?"

"I can't figure out how it opens."

Kid leaned over and flipped a hinge beneath the handles on each end of the trunk. "Now try it."

She pushed and easily opened the lid. Her expression of thanks stalled in her throat as the contents were revealed. Shimmering pink material, decorated with ruffles and delicate white lace was neatly folded across the top. With shaky fingers she touched the smooth, soft fabric.

"Pick it up. Let's see what it looks like."

"It's so beautiful," she whispered. Her eyes went to Kid. "Are you sure Stephanie said she didn't want this?"

"She said it's all stuff she's had lying around and will never wear. She was happy to get rid of it. Whatever doesn't fit you're suppose to put in a pile, and she'll help you alter it." Kid reached past her to lift the pink material out of the trunk.

As his arms rose, the material unfolded. The white lace circled a scalloped neckline, the edges of each sleeve, and ran along the bottom hem. Rows of pink ruffles ran up and down the bodice, from the waistline to the neckline.

"Oh!" It was the most beautiful dress she'd ever seen. Jessie reached out to touch it again.

Kid handed her the gown. "I'll leave you to try them on."

She nodded, speechless.

Chapter Eight

The calendar said September had arrived, and therefore, fall was on its way. Kid had believed it, but today the Kansas heat felt like a burning inferno, completely denying summer was slipping away. Sweat poured down his back and dripped from his armpits like spring rain.

"Kid, it's too damn hot to be out here today. One of us is gonna have a heatstroke. Probably me!" Joe reined his horse beside Jack. "It's not good for the cattle to move on a day like this either."

Kid removed his hat and wiped at the salty water trickling into his eyes. "Yeah, you're right. I didn't expect it to be this hot out here."

Joe's brows lifted with a surprised arch. "I'm right? I haven't heard that lately."

He ignored the comment, replaced his hat, and squinted at the herd. "Send the boys back to the ranch. I'll be along shortly."

"Kid-" Joe started.

Without waiting to hear what Joe had to say, he turned Jack and jarred him into an uneven trot. Joe's stare settled on his back, hotter than the sun. Damn this marriage thing had become harder than he thought it would be. Jessie had been cute enough in her ragged dress, but now, dressed in the assortment of gowns Stephanie had sent over, she was absolutely stunning. To the point it took his breath away at times.

He'd even ridden over and confronted his mother. Those were the best hand-me-downs he'd ever seen. Stephanie had confessed they were all new. Designs she'd created over the years. Unbeknownst to him, or the other boys, his mother had always wanted to be a dressmaker. Living in the middle of the prairie, where the closest town had fewer than fifty residents, hadn't hampered her passion. She'd gone ahead and created the gowns, claiming all along she knew someday she'd meet the woman she fashioned them for. Stephanie was ecstatic that woman had turned out to be his wife.

Kid wasn't.

Jack slowed to a walk. Kid lifted the canteen from the saddle horn and took a long swallow of the warm water. The horse stopped then slowly turned so his rump faced the blazing sun. Kid watched Joe signal the boys to halt the round up and head for the ranch.

He had to get away from her this morning and the allure of the sparkling blue gown she wore. The dress had an enticingly low neckline which emphasized she'd gained a few pounds. He almost groaned aloud, thinking about how her breasts had grown into round, luscious globes of delight. The enchanting gown fit her like a glove. His hands wanted to trace over the smooth contours. Even now, sitting in the hot sun, miles away from her, the thought made his loins ache with need. The last two weeks had been hell.

The smile that fell on him every time her magnetic blue eyes met his was pure and wholesome, and made his insides melt like butter in the sun. He couldn't find a fault in anything she did. Not her cooking, her cleaning, her intelligence, her willingness to please...nothing. Sammy, completely head over heels in love, wouldn't leave her side for the largest steak on earth.

Kid removed his hat again and used his arm to wipe at the sweat on his forehead.

Joe sent the last cowboy toward the ranch, then turned his mount and rode in Kid's direction. His pace slowed and came to a stop nearby.

"Want to rest a spell under that cottonwood 'afore we head back?" the man asked.

With a shrug, he nudged Jack toward a lone tree several yards away. Once under the cooling shade, he dismounted and dropped the reins to the ground. Joe followed suit.

Kid slipped the buttons of his shirt through the holes and pulled the wet material from his body. After using it to mop the sweat streaming down his torso, he flipped it over the back of saddle where the sun would dry it in no time.

"I don't really know why I decided these cows had to be moved today. It'll be a couple of months before they need to be closer to the ranch."

Joe nodded as he scraped at the ground with one boot. "Kid, I'm sorry for whatever I did to piss you off. If you tell me what it was, I'll make sure it doesn't happen again."

He moved to lean his back against the tree trunk and released a deep breath. "It wasn't anything you did. It's me. It's all me."

"What is it then? You sure have been acting out of sorts." Joe plucked a curled leaf and twirled the stem in his hand.

"I'm feeling out of sorts," he admitted. That damn little worm eating a hole in his stomach was the cause of it. The parasite was eating him from the inside out. Maybe talking to Joe would help. Nothing else had.

"Why's that?"

A false laugh rose from his chest. "My wife for one. First I have you sniffing around her skirts, and now I have my brothers."

"Sniffing around her skirts? What the hell are you talking about?" The leaf fluttered the ground. Joe crushed it with his boot.

He lifted his gaze. Joe's eyes glistened with anger. Kid's ire rose, whether at Joe, the little worm, or himself, he wasn't quite sure. "You didn't want her to think you were the 'bad guy'."

"Yeah, what about it? I think she's a sweet little gal." Joe's eyes widen and his mouth fell open. "You're in love with her, aren't ya?" His hand slapped Kid's shoulder. "Hot damn!"

"No, I'm not. I'm just trying to protect her, which has turned out to be more work than I thought." He moved away from the tall tree trunk and kicked at a pile of hard dirt stretching over a long root.

"Protect her from what?"

He turned to answer. What was he protecting Jessie from? Her brother? His brothers? Him?

Joe plucked another leaf, this time he stuck the stem in his mouth and chewed on it for a few minutes. "Kid, sometimes what one man has, ain't right for another man."

He scowled but waited for the man to go on.

"I know all these years you've been dreaming about having everything Sam Wharton had." Joe scratched his head. "Have you ever realized how things look a whole lot bigger and brighter when you're little? Maybe that rich rancher's place wasn't so big. And maybe his fancy wife wasn't so wonderful either. You were just a tyke when you stopped by his place with your Pa."

He turned and started walking toward Jack. This conversation would get him nowhere.

A hand fell on his arm. "Kid, don't walk away. What is it about Jessie you don't like?"

He shook the hand off and pulled his shirt from the saddle. Silence hung in the hot air. In the distance a bird chirped, the dried seed pod of a yucca plant rattled.

When he'd fastened the last button Kid let out a heavy sigh and admitted, "Nothing, there's nothing about Jessie I don't like."

"Then what's the problem?"

Kid mounted. "That is the problem." He turned Jack in the opposite direction from the ranch.

Joe nodded as if he understood. "Where're you going?"

He wished he understood. He looked at the hot sun and made a decision. "To Dodge. I'll go to see if any more drives are coming in this year."

"Want me to ride with you?"

"No."

"It's getting awfully late in the year for drives."

"Yeah, I know. Maybe someone got a late start out of Texas."

"How long you plan on being gone?" Joe reached into his saddlebag and pulled out a cloth sack.

Kid took it, knowing it held hard tack and jerky. Joe was always prepared. The man also handed him his canteen. After wrapping the leather strap around his saddle horn, he tucked the sack into his saddlebag.

"A few days."

"She'll be worried about you."

Kid pinched the bridge of his nose. "Keep an eye or her, Joe."

"I will. Be careful of riding too hard in this heat."

Kid nudged Jack forward. "I will."

****

Jessie glanced at the table set for two. Her heart landed in the pit of her stomach with a sad thud.

"He never said anything about needing to go to Dodge City. When did he decide to go?"

Joe didn't answer right away, just stood in the

doorway, one hand running up and down the doorframe.

"Today. He's checking to see if a late drive rolled in."

She pushed a clump of hair behind one ear. Had she done something wrong?

"He didn't say anything about it. Not this morning, not last night." Her feet stopped behind his chair. The wood felt cold beneath her fingers. "Hog shot a prairie chicken on his way over this morning. He showed me how to make dumplings. Said they're a favorite of Kid's."

"Hog?" Joe sounded surprised.

She clamped a hand over her mouth then nodded. Gloom had fuddled her mind. "Please don't say anything. I promised Hog I wouldn't, and he's been so good, teaching me how to cook and all."

"Hog's been showing you how to cook?" Joe's wide eyes held disbelief.

Jessie waved for him to step into the kitchen. "Promise you won't tell Kid?"

Joe closed the door behind him. His brow pulled down and caused more wrinkles to cover his tan forehead. "I-I promise."

Relieved to think of something besides Kid's absence, she said, "Hog loves to cook. Matter of fact, he does most of the cooking at his mother's. But Kid doesn't know about it. Hog's afraid he'd be mad. Stephanie swears by his cooking, which is why he's the one she sends over everyday to teach me." She laid a hand on Joe's forearm. "I promised him I wouldn't tell anyone."

"Don't fret, I won't tell anyone."

"Thank you. He's been so helpful and is a very patient teacher."

"You're still talking about Hog?"

She nodded. "He's going to be disappointed. He was excited to show me how to make the dumplings.

I'm supposed to tell him if Kid liked them." Steam rose from the kettle in the middle of the table, full to the brim of chicken, vegetables, thick gravy and fluffy, white dumplings. "I'll never be able to eat all this."

Joe scratched his cheek. "Well, if you don't want to eat alone, I could join ya."

"You will?" She clapped her hands. "Thank you. Please sit down. I never realized how sad it is to eat alone until I came to live here."

He took the chair she normally sat in. Her hand ran over the back of Kid's chair before she lowered onto it, and tried to absorb a feeling of his presence from the hard wood.

"There are biscuits under that cloth. Help yourself." Jessie filled both plates and passed one to Joe.

"Didn't you eat with your brother?"

"Excuse me?"

Joe chewed then swallowed. "Back at your place, I thought you lived with your brother. Didn't he eat with you?"

"Russell wasn't home very often. When he was…he'd usually already eaten."

From the way Joe ate, the meal had to be delicious. The food hit her stomach like stale bread. It wasn't eating alone that gave her a sad, sinking feeling, it was eating without Kid.

"Did he say how long he'd be gone?"

"Who?" Joe took another biscuit.

"Kid."

"Five days or so." He spoke around the food in his mouth.

"That long?"

A wide smile crossed his face, and he nodded like he knew something no one else did.

"What?" Jessie set her fork down.

"What, what?"

"I thought by the way you nodded you had something more to say."

"No, no, just that it takes that long to ride to Dodge and back."

"Oh." She picked the fork up and used it to shove the food around her plate. "I suppose I could go over and check the soddy while he's gone," she thought aloud.

"Uh?"

She sighed. "I claimed the land, I have to keep it up or I'll lose it." The fork clattered as it landed on the rim of her plate. Her chin fell to rest in the palms of her hands. "I'll have to move back there after Russell pays his debt."

Joe's mouth closed before his fork entered it. He lowered the food to his plate. "Why would you have to move back there?"

"Our marriage will end then."

"Huh?" He laid his fork down. "Your marriage to Kid?"

She nodded. "The preacher agreed it could end then." Another deep sigh left her lungs. The thought was excruciatingly sad. "So I should go check the soddy. Every time it rains the base crumbles and snakes find their way in. They're just bull snakes and mean no harm, but if the holes aren't fixed the whole bottom row of sod might let loose."

"I don't think Kid would like you going over there, but I tell you what, for sharing this here delicious meal with me, I'll take a couple of the boys and ride over there. We'll patch it up so you won't have nothin' to worry about." Joe picked up his fork and scooped the food into his mouth.

"Oh, would you? Thank you, Joe. That is so kind of you." She folded her hands in her lap, not really wanting to see the soddy. "Kid won't mind, will he?"

"Nope, matter of fact I think he'd like it." Joe swirled the last biscuit across the gravy on his plate before he popped it in his mouth.

"He will?"

"Yes, and he'll be awful sorry he missed this meal." He leaned back in his chair, patting his stomach with one hand. "Hog really cooked this meal?"

"I cooked it, but he told me how. He really is a fine cook. I've learned so much from him." Should she tell him the rest? Her mother had always called her a chatter box, but during the past several years she'd had no one to chat with. Could Joe keep two secrets? She hoped so.

Jessie leaned forward and whispered, "He and I are creating a cookbook. We are writing down his best recipes and when it's all done, we're going to send it to a publishing house in New York. I found the address in one of Kid's books. You won't tell him will you?"

Joe gave her a puzzled look. "Who? Kid?"

She nodded. "And please don't tell Hog I told you. His dream is to be a cook in a fancy restaurant like they have out east."

"Hog?" He scratched his head. "Guess I just never thought of him as the cooking type."

She rose to clear the table. "Well he is, and we made a deal, he'd teach me how to cook, and I'll write down all his recipes for his book." With both hands full she walked to the sink. Thinking of the Quinter brothers, a slight smile tugged on her cheeks. "They're all nice men when you get to know them."

Joe gathered other items off the table then carried them to her. "Who?"

"Hog, Snake, Bug, even Skeeter."

"And Kid?"

"Oh, he's definitely the nicest." Her cheeks burned. Sometimes her tongue was completely uncontrollable.

A chuckle filled the air. "Yes, he is the nicest." Joe cleared his throat. "Thank you, Mrs. Quinter for supper. I have to get out to the bunk house now. The boys are gonna think I forgot about them."

Jessie pretended to smooth the hair away from her face, while actually feeling to see if her cheeks were as hot on the outside as they were on the inside. Glad they were cool to the touch, she nodded, "I'm sorry I kept you from them, but I'm glad you ate supper with me."

"Any time." He retrieved his hat then walked to the door. "I'll let you know how it goes on the soddy."

"Thank you, Joe. Good night."

"Good night, Mrs. Quinter." A soft click echoed in the room.

Jessie stared at the door. Mrs. Quinter had such a lovely ring to it. All of the hands called her that and it never failed to send a warm, fuzzy feeling to flutter about in her insides.

The edge of her skirt pulled downward. One of Sammy's front paws rested on the hem. Big, round doggy eyes looked up at her. "Yeah, I miss him too." She wrapped both arms around the dog. "Funny, he wasn't here all day, and the house felt fine, but now that I know he's not coming home, it feels awfully empty." Sammy nudged his nose into her armpit for a deeper hug.

Jessie laid her head against his warm fur. Not once in the past two weeks had she thought about the little sod house, but tonight, hearing Kid wouldn't be home, reminded her the time at his ranch was temporary. In a matter of a few months this would all be gone- Sammy, the wonderful house, bountiful food, and worst of all, Kid. She'd no longer be Mrs. Quinter, but plain, old, Jessie Johnson again.

The heavy sigh tore at her lungs as she rose to her feet. Sammy curled near her ankles as she began to pump water into the sink for the dishes. There really was no hope of it being any different. She'd never be refined enough to be a rancher's wife, even after reading every book in his library, which would take her years. There were so many of them. Some of the ones she'd already read had been interesting, and others rather boring. Kid had said everyone has a choice, and her choice was to learn enough during her time here to guarantee she wouldn't have to rely on Russell when she moved back to the soddy. Her father had said book learning was extremely important, and surely there had to be something in one of those books that could make her self sufficient. If only there was something in the library to make her Kid's wife -forever.

Sammy's quick movements startled Jessie from her wondering thoughts.

Water overflowed the deep tub, dripping down the cupboard to where the dog had been lying. She reached down and pulled the plug, letting some water out. After wiping up the mess she'd made, she continued cleaning the kitchen.

"Come on, Sammy, you can have the rest of this, but you have to eat it on the porch." The dog followed her to the door, expectantly licking his lips as she poured the contents from the kettle into a large bowl near the steps.

She sat down, resting her feet on a lower stair, and stroked the black hair as the dog slurped at the food. A few men mingled about the barn, then started for the bunkhouse as Joe rang the iron triangle hanging from the shingled awning of the building. Russell wasn't among those walking across the yard. She hadn't seen much of him since the day Kid brought him home, but there was nothing new about that, she hadn't seen much of him the last few years- just when it was time to move on.

Jessie slapped her thighs and stood.

"No, no, I'm not going to dwell on that either. I have a few months to figure it all out, and I will figure it all out." Grabbing the empty kettle, she turned for the house. Kid's house. It would be so lonely without him. She'd become accustomed to sitting on the big divan reading while he worked in his office each evening after supper. Accustomed to the way he escorted her up to her room at bedtime, a familiar hand either holding her elbow or resting in the small of her back, the soft, warm kiss he always placed upon her forehead before leaving her outside her door.

He'd only kissed her, really kissed her, that one time. But she'd never forget it. In fact, she dreamed of it every night. The memory teased her mind as she went in to finish the dishes.

Would she be able to sleep, knowing he wasn't just down the hall? Jessie wiped the kettle dry and set it in the cupboard with others, blew out the lamps in the kitchen, and meandered through the foyer, pausing near the foot of the stairs. A dreadfully boring book about bovine disease awaited her on the table near one of the high-back chairs. Twisting around the staircase, she made her way down the hall to Kid's office, longing for something that would hold her interest on the lonely night.

Carefully, she searched the shelves, plucking and returning books to their slots. Near the bottom she found a stack of small, thick newspapers. She picked one up and held it closer to the lamp. A wide banner floated across the top of the page, *Waverly Library*. Scanning the front page, her heart began to pound. A black and white illustration portrayed a man holding a woman in a tight embrace, below the picture bold print said, *"Wholesome, Vigorous and Fresh."* Further down the publication claimed it covered the field of love and romance.

So excited she could barely breathe, Jessie

grabbed the rest of the stack and scurried from the room, Sammy close on her heels as she flew up the steps.

****

Kid spurred Jack until his hooves sent plumes of dust to trail behind them. Above, in a pure blue sky, lofty white clouds floated like puffs from a cottonwood tree. The sun, not yet high enough to blaze down unrelenting heat, sparkled in the east, and the early morning wind swirled around as if it had somewhere else to be and was late getting there. Kid pushed his hat further onto his head, upsetting the wind's attempt to take it.

A dust devil formed, picking up loose dirt and sand as it twirled across the prairie. He turned Jack away from the tiny twister's path. Once the miniature ground tornado, a common sight on the great flat land, whirled past he'd guide Jack back onto the well-worn trail.

He kept an eye out for rattlers, the snake that loved the harsh habitat, as he rode through a thick patch of goatheads. The small, thorned seed heads were a great nuisance and hurt like hell when you fell onto a patch of them. The irritating weeds could take over a field in no time. Constantly he pulled the hardy plants from the small garden he'd planted near the house.

Thoughts of the house brought his mind to Jessie. Hell, the blue sky, the lofty clouds, the miniature twister, the snakes, the weeds...everything reminded him of Jessie. He wasn't able to think of anything else. But the lone night on the prairie had given him some wisdom, and a plan. Why hadn't he thought of it sooner? Didn't matter, at some time during the lonely night, the ultimate solution had formed; an eastern boarding school. It would be expensive, but he'd find a way to afford it.

He ran a thumb and finger across his chin. "We just won't buy any winter calves."

Jack flipped his head around, as if questioning the words Kid had spoken aloud. With a click of his tongue, he urged the horse back to the trail, realizing the dust devil had long since twirled past.

"It'll work out, Jack." Was he trying to convince the horse, or himself?

The low bawling of cattle mingled with the whistling of the wind. Dark humps on the horizon grew into a herd as they drew closer. Kid reined Jack to the left, bypassing the cattle as they rode the last few miles into Dodge City. Within no time, the town rose up out of the barren ground to surround him with saloons, mercantile stores, hotels, and the hustle and bustle of the city.

A train whistle sliced the air. The town had passed an ordinance- no guns could be worn north of the tracks, the respectable part of town. However, on the south side, anything went. Kid pulled the pistol from his holster and buried it in his saddle bag as he made his way to Front Street.

Bawdy voices and loud music wafted through the swinging doors of the many saloons lining the boardwalk on both sides of the well-worn road. He steered Jack through the traffic, toward the telegraph office, the best place to look for eastern newspapers. Dismounting, he flipped a rein over the post, straightened his shirt, and resettled his hat before making his way onto the boardwalk.

A bell chimed above his head, bringing the gaze of the man behind the desk his way.

"Well, hey, Kid." Adam Zimmerman stood and extended his hand. "Weren't you just in town a couple weeks ago?"

"Adam." Kid shook the hand. "Yeah, I was, but forgot to follow up on something. Do you have a copy of the *New York Times* I could look at?"

"Sure, there's a stack over there." Adam pointed at a table between two chairs. "Go ahead and take what you need. I save them for winter fires and such."

"Thanks." Kid went to the table as another customer walked in. He let out a sigh of relief, not wanting to explain what he looked for. Adam would learn soon enough. Filtering through the papers, a headline jumped from the page.

"The Woman's University. A Model College for the Higher Education of Women..." He sat down and read the article word for word. Located fifteen miles outside of Boston, the school promised to put sound minds inside strong bodies, using honor, not the strict statutes of some other mentioned establishments. He raised an eyebrow as he read some of the other schools didn't allow the girls to correspond with home, cross liberties, or speak with any men for the three years they resided there. The article went on to say at the Woman's University, the four hundred girls in attendance were too busy with the great possibilities of education and the prospect of future usefulness to have much thought of the other sex.

He lowered the paper to his lap. What would Jessie think of this? Would she fit in with the other three hundred and ninety-nine girls? He twisted his shoulders against a shudder. That was a hell of a lot of women.

"Find what you were looking for, Kid?" Adam asked from the counter.

Kid glanced around the office, finding it empty, he rose and crossed the floor. "Could you send a telegram to this place? Ask if they have any openings and how much it costs?"

Adam pulled the paper over and read. "The Women's University?"

Kid shuffled his stance. "Yeah, it's, uh, it's for a

friend of mine."

"Sure, Kid, it'll cost ya twenty-five cents."

"That's the going price for everything in Dodge, isn't it?" Kid joked, hoping to take the man's mind off his request.

"Yup, a shave, a drink, a needle, ain't nothing that costs less than a quarter," Adam said as he gathered the coins off the counter. "Where do I send the response?"

"I'll be at the Dodge House for a day or so, I'll stop by before I leave town."

"Sounds good." Adam put the paper on his desk and sat down to create the message.

Kid left the building deep in thought. Was sending Jessie away the best answer? A dark cloud overtook his senses. Like a storm building ferocity to rip across the plains. He glanced to the sky- brilliant blue, not a thunderhead in sight. The heavy, murky aura came from the inside out, and was a complete contrast to what he'd felt lately. For as much as he tried to ignore the truth, the fact was since she'd moved in, his world had been altered. It was as if the sun had been awakened within his soul. A bright, warm light he'd never experience had been turned on and shone inside his body, creating a feeling of overwhelming elation.

Whether he was willing to admit it or not, each day he had counted the hours until he'd arrive home again and she'd greet him with a smile as pure as paradise. He leaned against the hitching post. Jack, tied on the other side, patiently waited.

The hot heat of midday, the out of tune piano playing across the street, the shouts of passerby's, none of it lessened the way his body responded to thoughts of her. Remembering how sweet she smelled, how soft she felt, how lovely she looked, made his toes curl.

The hand landing on his shoulder pulled him

out of la la land. He twisted, ready to snap at the intruder. Catching the shiny glint from the six-pointed star pinned on the man's shirt, he swallowed the retort.

"Kid Quinter, what are you doing back in town so soon?" George Hinkle had defeated Bat Masterson last fall for the position of the Ford County Sheriff. Ironically, he was another person Kid wanted to track down while in town.

"Just a little business to take care of, part of it includes talking to you." He pushed away from the post, taking the proffered hand in a friendly shake. George had been a bartender at Hoover's Saloon for years, Kid knew him well.

"Really? Well, come on, I'll buy you a drink as we talk," Hinkle offered.

Kid followed the sheriff off the boardwalk and fell into step as they walked across the street. "How are things going?"

"The usual." Hinkle shrugged and pointed to one of the several saloons lining the opposite side of Front Street. Since over twenty establishments in the cow town were licensed to sell liquor, it wasn't hard to find a quiet corner in one.

"So what's up?" Hinkle asked as he waved to a barkeep and walked toward the back of the building.

Kid remained silent and followed George to one of the small round tables.

A weary and strained looking woman set two glasses, sloshing with bronze liquid, in front of them. A moment later she returned with a full bottle of the popular brew. Her gaze lingered on him for a moment. Her stained, red dress looked as if she'd slept in it. She winked at him before turning away. The dark circles under her eyes made him wonder if sleep was the right word. He twisted his neck against the tension creeping in. Sending Jessie to Boston was the best thing. The Kansas plains had little to offer young women. Wrapping his fingers around the glass in front of him, he lifted his gaze to Hinkle.

The sheriff had a brow raised.

"Have a drifter out at my place, wondering if you've heard of him." Kid swallowed the shot of whiskey. Hot fire streamed down his throat, exploding in his stomach like a stick of dynamite. A fleeting thought left him hoping the potent brew might kill the nasty little worm who'd taken up residence deep in his guts. He smacked his lips as he set the glass down.

"What's his name?" George asked as he refilled his glass and Kid's.

"Russell Johnson."

Chapter Nine

Hinkle stopped the glass near his mouth. Eyebrows arched as he set his drink down. "Yeah, I've heard of him. Send him on his way."

Kid ran a finger over the rim of his glass. "Is there a warrant out on him?"

"Not officially, but there should be." Hinkle tossed the bronze liquid into his mouth, gritting his teeth as he swallowed.

He took a sip out of his glass, letting the strong taste roll across his tongue for a moment. "Tell me about it."

"Well, there's not much to tell. The man and his younger sister lived in a tent on the south side. I never saw the sister, or Johnson, actually, but I had plenty of reports on the little scheme going on. Johnson made the rounds, talking up his virgin little sister."

His stomach began to roll. He'd felt this way once before- when Aunt Bonnie told him his mother was gone. Not dead, just gone. It was later he learned they meant the same thing. An empty, indescribable sensation had twisted his guts, filling the area with tiny, sharp pinches. Just like the ones plucking at him now. Bile rose into the back of his throat. He took a breath, not a cleansing one, but one like a drowning man would take before slipping back beneath the water. One needed for survival.

Russell was trouble; he had no doubt about that, but not Jessie. She was an innocent bystander. That little worm from his stomach must have made its way to his brain where it nudged him to wonder. *Wasn't she?* Kid pulled his hand away from his glass and waved for Hinkle to continue.

The sheriff twirled his glass on the table. "He promised her body to many, got 'em liquored up, then took them back to their tent where he'd knock 'em in the head and roll them for their money. Most of them were cattle boys, in town with a drive. They'd complain to me, but they'd been so drunk they couldn't remember what he looked like, or where the tent was. Part of the problem was Johnson wasn't the only one doing it. Plenty of the vagrants pull the same scheme. It's nothing new." He lifted the glass to his lips. "You've seen the south side, the hundreds of tents out there?"

Kid nodded. Below the table, his hands balled into fists so tight his wrists throbbed. His temples pulsed with each beat of his heart. Were the men knocked in the head before or after they slept with Jessie? How had he been so stupid? Believing her act of innocence, thinking the way she responded to his kiss that night back at the ranch had been instinct, not learned from years of practice at seduction.

Hinkle shook his head. "Well, they finally got caught. Rolled the wrong man."

He clenched his back teeth. His family always claimed his anger would kill someone. Maybe they were right. But who would it be? Russell? The men Jessie had been with? Hinkle for being the messenger? Jessie?

The pressure on his molars made his jaw begin to hurt. He opened his mouth and threw the liquid in his glass against his burning throat. An invisible, heavy weight pushed on his shoulders. Keeping his voice as even as possible, he asked, "What happened?"

"Jed Montgomery happened. He's a gunslinger from New Mexico, works for Ted Hughes. He's a mean one, but hasn't done anything I can arrest him for. Even checks his guns at the rail line. Johnson laid Montgomery's head wide open then hauled him to the edge of the tent city. I thought Jed would kill the man for sure." Hinkle shrugged. "Actually, I hoped he would- kill two birds with one stone, make my job easier. But Johnson was a slick one, kept a few steps ahead of Montgomery for a week or so, then after Jed cornered the sister one day, Johnson and the gal left town. Jed's still screeching about it."

Kid tried to keep his nostrils from flaring. "What did Montgomery do to the sister, when he cornered her?"

"Poor thing." George shook his head.

Kid's heart stopped dead.

Hinkle continued, "An old wash nag claims the girl didn't know anything about what her brother was doing. Said the sister worked all day, every day, trying to earn a touch of coin by washing clothes for the drivers and such. I guess a couple others at the camp stopped Montgomery from hurting the girl too bad. No one would admit much, but my guess is they found a wagon heading west for her to catch a ride on, and since Russell disappeared at the same time, I assumed he'd gone with her." He swallowed another shot of whiskey then asked, "Is the sister with him at your place?"

She didn't have anything to do with Russell's scam. He hadn't been duped. Isn't that what he just heard? His breath caught. Or had Jessie duped the others at the tent city as well? He looked at Hinkle. The man stared at him expectantly. Kid's mind was too befuddled to do anything but nod.

"Is it true?"

Kid frowned, blinked. Tried to clear his mind.

"Is what true?"

"Jed, as well as the men at the tent city, say she's the prettiest thing they'd ever laid eyes on." Hinkle's voice held a touch of skepticism. "Is she?"

Visions filled his head- Jessie, strolling down the wide staircase, sauntering across the kitchen with long, silky waves of golden-brown hair swaying in her wake. Pale blue eyes, sparkling with delight, and pert, pink lips smiling as she greeted his entrance. A shimmering light flickered inside him. He couldn't see it, but felt it nonetheless. Her soft giggles echoed somewhere in the back of his mind. His nose twitched, recalling the clean, fresh scent of her skin. He ran his tongue over his lips, against the itch. They seemed to long for the smooth warmth of her forehead. The spot he kissed each night before she went to bed- the one self indulgence he'd allowed. He took a breath as his body heat rose-from the inside out. Like the sun rising in the east, light filled his soul. He couldn't describe the feeling settling in his chest. Happiness at knowing Jessie was innocent? Perhaps. If so, why did his mind still feel heavy with dread?

"Is she?" Hinkle asked again.

Kid downed the bronze liquid in his glass. The little worm had slithered back into his gut, but it had matured into a full grown snake, coiled and ready to strike. He took a moment to ponder it. Jessie was innocent, he had no doubt. She was too pure, too untainted to have been with other men. Then why did he still want to kill someone? Why did he feel more jealous of her than he had of anything in his life? He reached for the bottle of whiskey. "Yeah. She's the prettiest thing I've ever seen."

Hinkle sighed as if he'd just opened his canteen and found it empty. He sat back in his chair, folded his arms. "She work for you too?"

"No."

"But you've seen her?"

Kid filled both of their glasses, swallowed his in one gulp. Snake or no snake, a smile tugged at his lips. The dim room grew brighter. He shrugged the imagined weight of his shoulder and slapped the glass onto the table.

"I married her."

Wide-eyed with shock, George stared across the table. "No shit?"

****

Jessie listened carefully as Snake explained, "The weeping willow tree is very remarkable. It has more nutrients and natural fertilizer than any other plant known to man. The juices of the branches mingle with the water, producing nourishment that stimulates growth in anything you pour it on. And, if we continue to plant the left over mush, within a few years you'll have enough trees to have a garden twice this size, besides the cooling shade the trees will provide. Kid's lucky to have such good ground water. Willows need lots of water."

With a small axe Snake cut the long, limber branches into small chunks. The pieces fluttered off the chopping block to the ground near his boots. He and Hog weren't tall and gangly like Skeeter. They were taller than she, but stocky. With light brown hair and happy green eyes, the brothers were nice looking, and she'd come to depend on each of them immensely. Even Skeeter had proven invaluable when it came to keeping her wood box full. He stopped by every few days with another load of dried wood he'd found here or there.

When the chopping stopped she said, "I can't believe how much the plants have grown since you made that first tub of water for me."

"Yes, it is amazing, isn't it?" His eyes went to the vegetable plants behind them. "With these additional four barrels, you'll have enough juice to fertilize every other day." He separated the chopped branches and leaves then began to place them in the bottom of the large rain barrels he'd made.

Jessie dumped water on top of the branches out of the buckets Bug carried from the well. She smiled her thanks at the youngest brother then turned to Snake and asked, "When can I use the water from these barrels?"

"The clippings have to sit in the water for at least twenty-four hours, and make sure you never use all the water from any of the tubs. Just a couple buckets full and make sure you refill the tubs afterwards. They'll last a couple of weeks, then we'll plant the clippings and you'll have another tree." Snake turned to Bug and asked, "Have you dug the holes?"

Snake had an incredible knowledge of gardening. Each day, after Hog gave her a cooking lesson, she spent hours with Snake, tending the small garden Kid had planted. The first day he'd shown her how to crush old buffalo bones and sprinkle it amongst the plants, after that he had her start watering the plants with the mixture he created from willow branches. Now, she not only had vegetables to cook, but also enough to put up for winter, and Snake said he'd plant the used clippings, swearing willow trees would grow from the mulch.

"Yup, four of them just like you said, two behind the house and one on each side," Bug said, his smile growing wide as he turned to her. "Kid's gonna be happy about the trees. Don't you think so, Jessie?"

She patted his arm. "Yes, Bug. I'm sure Kid will like the trees." The boys never ceased to amaze her at how they all wanted to please their older brother.

"When's he coming home, Jessie?" Bug asked.

A little sigh escaped and she shrugged.

"He's only been gone three days, Joe said it would be five or so," she answered, feeling as sad as

Bug looked.

She could relate closest with the youngest brother, they both felt as if Kid had hung the sun in the sky himself. For her, he truly had, he'd rescued her from darkness and provided light. If only she could find a way to stay here with him forever. If only Kid would fall in love with her like the men in the wonderful, romantic stories she read in the *Waverly Library* newspapers. Each addition held a lengthy novel, full of tales of men and women falling helplessly in love, and living happily ever after. After reading the first story, Jessie made a couple more choices, one: to read the rest of the stack, and two: to find love like the heroines. She just had to figure out a way to make Kid love her like the heroes loved the heroines.

"Bug and I will plant the trees, Jessie. You can go on into the house, get out of the sun for awhile," Snake said.

Snapped out of her wondering thoughts, she waved a hand over her heated cheeks.

"Thanks, Snake, it is awfully warm out here. Come in for some cookies I made before you two leave for home."

The boys agreed and she left them to walk to the house. Sammy, as usual, ambled beside her knee, stopping now and again when an interesting smell caught the attention of his long snout. She'd pause and wait for him to catch up before moving forward again, happy to have him for a constant companion.

The sun had fallen low in the sky; signaling the day would soon end. It was of little consequence, without Kid home to eat she hadn't bothered planning a meal. A piece of bread would be plenty for her and Sammy had already eaten the left over beans from last night. She reached down and patted his round stomach as they walked up the stairs.

The dog leaped in front of her and let out a low

growl as she opened the back door. She scanned the room, her gaze stopping when her heart flew into her throat. Jessie squared her shoulders, patted the dog on the head then stepped into the room.

"What do you want?"

His mouth gapped open. "Is that anyway to treat your brother? You've barely acknowledged I'm alive the past two weeks," Russell whined.

Sammy snarled, showing long teeth as Russell rose from Kid's chair at the end of the table. She ran a hand over the dog's head, but didn't quiet him.

"Perhaps I don't care if you're alive or not."

Russell glanced from the dog to her. "Tell him to shut up. We need to talk."

She let out a sigh, folded her arms across her chest and thought about his request for a moment. The dog's low growls and ornery yaps made thinking hard.

"Sammy, shush. Sit." The dog kept his eyes on Russell, but stopped snarling. His wide, black rump landed on both of her feet.

"I don't have anything to say to you." Thankful for the dog's protection, she was able to focus on her choice, the one where Russell would never interfere with her life again.

Russell gave a look of disbelief. "What? Nothing to say to me? Don't you want to thank me? Don't you think my plan is working out well? I had this all planned, Jessie. I knew you'd never survive a winter in that crumbling soddy. I knew I had to find you a fine house to live in, and I did, didn't I? This is just about the finest house I've ever seen. I've always taken care of you, haven't I Jessie? I've never let any real harm come to you. Did you think it would be any different this time?"

Her mind swirled. Russell had a way of twisting everything until she saw it his way. She pressed a hand to her forehead.

He smiled, his eyes connecting with hers. "Can't you see everything I've done was for you? Didn't I promise you all of this? A house, beautiful clothes, plenty of food."

She closed her eyes, shutting out his mesmerizing gaze.

"Jessie, look at me. It's me, your brother, the only kin you have. The only one who cares about you," he coaxed.

Both hands covered her eyes, forcing them not to open and look at him. Anxiety rose. She had to think. Think beyond his persuading tone.

"I've done everything for you, and here you are not willing to help me at all."

Kid. She had to think of Kid, he could block any other visions from her mind. She pulled her hands away, balling them into fists as they fell to her sides and glared at her brother.

"Not do anything for you? I think keeping your neck from being stretched is something." The weight lifted off her feet. As if Sammy could sense her frustration, the dog stood, snarling at Russell while the hairs on his back popped to stand on end and form a long trail down his silky back.

"Jessie, that was all part of my plan," Russell cooed. "And now it's time for the second part to start."

"The second part?" she wondered aloud.

"Yes, look at you. You have everything you need. But look at me, I'm living in a bunk house, eating scraps not fit for the dog that's always at your feet. I have to work from sun up to sun set, while you're living the life of luxury. It's not fair, Jessie. The brother of a rich rancher's wife is a prominent position. I should be helping with the books, taking trips to buy and sell cattle, making deals with the railroad to ship our cattle."

Her brain started to fuzz over again. "Our

cattle?"

"Yes, our cattle. Everything here is half yours. And since I'm your brother, half of yours is mine."

She shook her head, needing to see and hear clearly. "No, it's not. It's not yours, and it's not mine. It's Kid's. He's worked hard to build what he has. Why, he even built this whole house by himself." A sense of pride at her husband's accomplishments filled her chest.

"And he's married to you. If something were to happen to him, as his wife, it would all be yours."

A shiver rose up her spine. The muscles in her neck tightened, making it hard to breathe. A lump stuck in her throat.

"No. No, Russell. Oh, God, what have you done?"

"Done? I haven't done anything, yet. And if you want to keep it that way, you'll talk to your husband when he returns, and convince him how smart I am. How I could be more help to him than a simple cow hand."

A small bit of relief oozed from her pores. Russell had been around the past few days, she'd seen him now and again, so he couldn't have harmed Kid. The thought was also like a splash of cold water making her thoughts clear again.

"No, Russell. I've made a choice. I'll never be a part of one of your schemes again."

He gave her a look laced with disgust. "You've made a choice? What the hell is that supposed to mean?"

The red haze of anger floated before her eyes. "It means I don't have to do what you say. I'm eighteen. I can make my own decisions and live my own life, one that doesn't revolve around you. Get out, Russell, get out of my house!" She pointed to the back door.

"Your house? You just said this isn't your house. It's Kid's." His eyes narrowed into slits. He stared at her for a long moment.

"You know what Jessie? You're right. It's not your house, and it never will be. As soon as Kid Quinter has extracted his money from me, he'll kick you out. Back to the snake infested shanty you'll go. It'll be the dead of winter, and you won't have any wood, any food, not even have a blanket to keep you warm."

"Kid won't do that. He's a kind man. I know he'll help me," she argued, her voice rising close to a scream.

Russell's voice, laced with anger rose above hers. "Why? Why should he help you? You're not the wife he wants. Ask any of his brothers, they'll tell you, he's planning on going to Europe to find a beautiful, refined woman to be his wife. The kind of woman a rich rancher needs."

Her knees grew weak, trembling beneath her skirt like wheat heads in the wind.

He continued his loud rant, "He's already got the trip paid for, leaving right after the first of the year. Why would he want to help some scrawny, homely, orphan prostitute? He'll have no use for you. You better hope your evening activities don't land you in the family way. Then you'll really be up a creek without a paddle, nothing more than a used up whore with a squalling bastard to take care of."

Before Jessie could respond, the back door slammed open.

Bug flew past her, knocking Russell and the chair over backwards as he screamed, "Don't talk to Jessie like that!"

Arms and legs flew in all directions as the two rolled across the floor, fists slammed at each other and legs kicked. Sammy's barks grew loud as he leaped around them, teeth nipping at pant legs and arm sleeves.

Coming out of shock, and not knowing what else

to do, Jessie screamed, "Bug! Sammy!"

Another body rushed past yelling, "Get her the hell out of here!"

"Kid?" She recognized the voice the same moment solid arms wrapped around her waist. Someone lifted her feet from the floor and turned to haul her towards the door. She twisted and bucked, trying to see who held her. "No! Put me down!"

The arms around her waist tightened.

Scratching at the hands locked on her stomach, she kicked in protest as crashing noises behind her mingled with shouts, grunts and barks.

"Put me down!"

A grunt sounded as her heel met a knee cap. "Ouch, Jessie, calm down," Snake's voice sounded next to her ear.

She eased her fighting as Snake carried her across the yard. Near the well he set her feet on the ground. Ready to run back to the house, she turned but firm hands landed on her shoulders. "Kid will handle it, Jessie," he said.

"Kid's home?" She twisted, searching over Snake's shoulder.

"Yes, he's home. He'll handle it. You just stay here with me."

The back door hung at an odd angle. Banging, clanging and loud barks continued to float through the open area.

"Snake, Bug's in there." Tears began to flow. "I have to go help him." She pushed at the arms holding her in place and tried to twist away.

His solid grasps didn't lessen as he shook his head. "Kid won't let anything happen to Bug."

Joe and a couple other men ran across the yard and onto the porch. Snake turned her around, and with an arm across her shoulders, refused to allow her to look toward the house. He tried to ease her mind, making her walk further away from the house. "Do you want to go see where we planted the trees?" he asked.

"No!"

"It's not far. One is just right over there." Snake continued to refuse to allow her to turn around.

"No! I don't want to see any trees." Tears burned her eyes. "I want to go see if Bug's all right. I want..." A sob escaped as she admitted, "I want Kid."

Snake wrapped his other arm around her and pressed her face onto his chest. "Shh, in a minute, Jessie, you'll see Kid in a few minutes."

Her chest burned, and her head pounded with pain, uncontrollable weeping made every ache worse. The arms around her shoulders lessened. A swift movement twisted her around and a familiar scent filled her nostrils as a firm hold guided her face to once again press against a male chest. Gentle hands rubbed her shoulders and ran down her back, folding her curves against hard contours she'd felt before. She wrapped her arms around Kid's waist, clinging to the sculptured form.

"Shh, sweetheart, don't cry." The brush of warm breath tickled her ear.

"Kid?" She tried to lift her head, needing to make sure it was him, but a strong hand held it in place.

"Yes, it's me. And I won't let anyone hurt you ever again." Lips touched the top of her head.

A moan bubbled out her throat, the warm, caring embrace shattering any bits of control she had left. Kid was home. She went limp, melting against his strength.

Her feet rose from the ground. One strong arm wrapped beneath her knees while the other encompassed her shoulders, Kid cradled her as a mother would a crying infant. Her arms went around his neck and her face pressed against the warm skin near the top of his shirt, where his scent could fill each intake of breath.

Kid carried her around the house. They entered through the front door, his long strides taking the stairs two at a time. He weaved through the great room and climbed the inside set of stairs. When his body lowered, he cuddled her on his lap, swaying back and forth while filling her ears with soft words of comfort.

It wasn't until the tears stopped flowing, and she lifted her head, did she realize he'd carried her into her bedroom. She wiped at her face, using the sleeve of her dress to dry the moisture. Not sure if she'd been crying because of Russell, or the fear of Bug being hurt, or the fact that Kid was home.

"I'm sorry, Kid. I'm so sorry," she choked.

"Shh, you didn't do anything," he whispered.

She'd missed him so much, missed that handsome, gentle face looking down at her. She lifted her hand to press a palm against the rough growth of whiskers covering his cheek, and looked deep into dark, intense eyes, wishing she could read his thoughts.

His face lowered. The soft touch of his lips stole her breath away. She tried to think, wanting to remember how the women in the stories responded to kisses. But the soft, warm, wet lips roaming over hers sent hot, sizzling sparks throughout her body, dissolving her thoughts.

Sweet, fulfilling nectar quenched his thirst, flowing through his body hotter and faster than any amber liquor he'd ever tasted. Kid licked at the tonic, swallowing each drop, wanting more and more with each taste. His hands moved swiftly, roaming over contours he'd only dreamed of exploring.

The soft mattress floated up to surround their bodies as he slipped her off his lap so they could recline, giving room for deeper and more thorough discoveries. Kid, positioned above her frame, forced his hands to slow so he could stroke the soft curves, appreciating each inch, while savoring the deep, sensual kisses. The small, searching hands flowing over his back and neck sent additional rivers of pleasure through his body.

Something tugged his leg, he kicked at the intrusion, but it came again, this time with more force. Opening one eye, he peeked at the invasion. Sammy's teeth clutched the cuff of his pant leg. The dog tugged again, his front paws braced against the side of the mattress. Kid tried to pull the material from the dog's mouth. A low growl emitted as Sammy tightened his hold.

The soft lips moving below his stilled and brought his full attention back to the woman beneath him. Dark lashes, fluttered. He pressed one last kiss across the moist lips, and with a wide smile, waited for her eyes to open. His heart pounded harder than a stampede of Texas longhorns.

The warmth of a small palm cupped his jaw, one fingertip ran along the healed scratched on his cheek. "I missed you," she whispered.

The sound filled him with a new wave of gratification. "I missed you too, sweet Jessie." He had. Three days away from her had felt like three years. Poor Jack, he'd pushed the horse hard the final ten miles of the trip an unexplainable urgency overriding common sense.

A long, black chin settled itself on the mattress near her shoulder. A wet nose sniffed her dress as worried brown eyes looked at them. Her smiling face turned to glance at the dog.

"Hi, Sammy," she said.

His tail thumped the floor, much like the rhythm pounding in Kid's chest. A twinge, similar to a snake bite bit in the same area. Jealousy? Could a man be jealous of a dog? Or was it irritation at being so rudely interrupted?

The soft gaze of the blue eyes became shadowed, turning to worry, or fear as they wandered back to meet his. "Is-" she paused to swallow. "Is Bug all right?"

Wrapping his hand around the fingers settled on his cheek, he kissed each knuckle, regretting how reality had settled in the room.

"Yes, Bug is fine."

Her brows furrowed and her eyes squeezed shut. "I'm so sorry, so very sorry."

Forgotten fury began to renew itself. Holding it in check, he pulled his body upright, bringing hers with him.

As they settled on the edge of the bed, Sammy laid his head across her skirt and released a small whimper, as if he too apologized. Neither of them had anything to be sorry for, it was that damned brother. If Joe hadn't stepped in when he did, Kid would have killed the man. His fingers tingled, recalling how close they'd come to squeezing Russell's neck.

He tugged Jessie's head onto his shoulder, bending to press his lips against her temple. "You didn't do anything wrong."

"But he's my brother, and..." A deep sigh made her shoulders slump. "I don't know how to make him behave."

"It's not up to you to make him behave. You have no more control over your brother than I have over mine," he said.

Her head tilted so she could look up at him. A deep frown pulled at her brows and her lips puckered. "But your brothers are good boys. They've helped me so much since I came to live here."

The recollections of how the boys had bound and gagged him didn't increase his anger, instead a glow of delight settle somewhere in his chest. Their actions that night had brought her to him. He smiled and said, "Yeah, they can be good boys." For no reason, other than wanting to erase the pained look on her precious face, he added, "Just as I'm sure your brother can be once in awhile."

She shook her head. "Not very often...I can't think of one time right now."

"Then let's not think of him right now." He would have to deal with Russell soon enough, and needed time to decide what he would do with the irredeemable bastard. Recalling her words, a deeper frowned formed on his brows.

"What have my brothers done to help you?"

Her cheeks tinged pink. "Everything, they've helped me water the garden, brought me recipes from Stephanie, carried in wood for the stove, shot game, planted trees..."

"They've done all that?"

She nodded. "Everyday at least one of them shows up to help with some chore or another."

"Hmm. Well, it's about time those boys grow up." He assumed his brothers were coming over everyday just to irritate him, but now that he thought about it, they did always seem to be busy whenever he caught sight of them.

Her hand stroked the back of Sammy's head, shapely nails scratching behind the dog's ears. The whiteness of her skin reminded him of the grit covering his body after spending three days plagued by the Kansas wind. The water might also wash away some of the other strain plaguing his body.

He took her hand, pushed Sammy's head from her lap, and said, "Have you tried out any new recipes lately? I'm ready for some supper and a hot bath."

She jumped to her feet, a smile forming on her lips. "Yes, I made some molasses cookies this morning. They're quite tasty."

Kid rose. The happiness in her eyes made his heart patter. He massaged the fine bones in her hand with big, callused fingertips. He placed a soft kiss on her lips and said, "I'm sure they are."

Chapter Ten

Three days later, Jessie still couldn't help but wonder what had happened to Russell. She hadn't seen neither hide nor hair of him since Bug had flown into the house. On the other hand, the Quinter brothers were all fine. They each had stopped by to see how she was, and talked with Kid, for a significant amount of time. A sigh of pleasure left her chest. The mere thought of her husband shattered away any worries of Russell.

She pressed a hand against the thumping behind her breastbone, remembering the long, sensual kiss they'd shared before he left the kitchen this morning. Since his trip to Dodge, Kid had taken to kissing her on the lips, often. She had read and reread every sensual passage from the stack of papers beside her bed, hoping to find a way to make Kid happy, make him love her. So far the novels had been very little help.

A loud knock sounded on the front door, startling her to the point the flour cup slipped from her fingers. A cloud of white erupted around her feet and the clang of metal rang out as the tin came to rest near the table leg. The knock grew to a pound as she quickly stepped over the mess, and fluffing the white powder from the bottom of her yellow skirt made her way through the kitchen.

Sammy, teeth bared, stepped in front of her as

she opened the glass paned front door. The man on the stoop took a step back as the dog shot forward, nipping at the sheriff's knees.

"Damn it! Call that critter off!" Sheriff Turley shouted, taking another step back and catching himself with the square pillar before falling off the stoop.

"Sammy! Be good!" Jessie said.

Sammy turned and gave her a big doggy grin, letting her know he was only pretending. A smile tugged at the corners of her mouth before she looked back up to the man.

"Hello, Sheriff."

"Where's Kid?" he asked.

She shrugged and answered, "Out checking cattle. Is something wrong?"

"No." With a weary glance toward the dog sitting on her toes, the sheriff reached forward, handing her a slip of paper. "This telegram came for him."

Sammy let out a low growl as she took the paper. The sheriff quickly pulled his empty hand away. As the man's hand fell to his side, a horse flew around the side of the house and skidded to a halt near the steps.

Kid dismounted and bounded up the few stairs. "Turley, what do you want?" he asked as he brushed past the man, his eyes searching her.

One arm settled around her shoulders. "Are you all right?"

"Yes, yes, I'm fine. Sheriff Turley brought this out to you." She snuggled in beneath his arm and handed him the note.

His arm tightened as he gave her a little nod before he turned to the sheriff, stuffing the paper in his shirt pocket.

"Thanks, Turley."

"Looks like things are going pretty good out

here." Sheriff Turley glanced at the arm around her shoulder before he looked at Kid.

"Yes, things are going just fine," Kid said. The hand cupping her upper arm ran up and down, the friction warm and comforting.

As if it had a mind of its own, her arm snuck around his back. Her hand folded over a lean, solid hip. His fingers slipped from her arm to her rib cage, making her breasts tingle with anticipation as he rubbed the area directly below them. A slow grin touched his lips and one eye fluttered a wink. Her heart turned a somersault and came to rest against the wall of her chest, pounding against her ribs like a chicken pecking grit.

"Yeah, well, uh, you got a minute, Kid?" The sheriff's words pulled Kid's eyes from hers and broke the spell she was under.

A long sigh left his chest before Kid answered, "Sure." He glanced back down at her. "Jessie, do you have any coffee made? Maybe a few of those molasses cookies to go with it?"

She nodded, a frown forming at the thought of the mess she'd left in the kitchen.

"Could you please bring some to my office?" he asked.

"Yes, yes, of course." She let out a sigh, thankful he wouldn't see the kitchen.

After serving the men, she went about cleaning up her mess and finishing the batch of bread the sheriff's arrival had interrupted. Her mind wandered, both to what the sheriff wanted, and about how wonderful Kid made her feel. The warmth of her cheeks had little to do with the heat of the day as she kneaded eggs into the dough.

An hour or so later, while she laid a cloth over the dough filled pans, long arms snaked around her waist and pulled her back against a firm body. She patted the hands below her breasts, enjoying the shivers of pleasure each and every embrace from Kid provided. The blissful sensations allowed her to relate to the heroines of the love tales. Slipping to her hips, his hands turned her around before they spread to her back, holding her close as his lips met hers.

Jessie kissed him back, knowing at this moment in time, she held everything she'd ever wanted, would ever need. It still amazed her at how quickly he'd turned her life around. Couldn't believe how she'd become so lucky.

Kid pulled his lips from hers. His heart raced faster than a jack rabbit chased by a coyote. He kissed her forehead before folding her face into the hollow of his neck. The arms wrapped around his waist helped to calm the raging anger and fear filling his body.

Usually he wouldn't have given Turley the time of day, but once he'd realized Jessie was safe, he'd felt generous. That had been before Turley said George Hinkle sent a message to his office, asking him to warn Kid that Jed Montgomery had left Dodge. The man was hell bent on finding Russell- and Jessie.

Keeping her in his embrace, where she was safe, Kid pressed a cheek to the top of her head, and hoping she wouldn't sense his anxiety, whispered, "Thank you for the coffee and cookies. As usual, they were very good."

His hand remained firm, not allowing her to lift her face when she tried. He couldn't take the chance of her seeing concern in his eyes.

Warm, sweet breath tickled his neck when she answered, "You're welcome."

A few minutes later, he relaxed his hold and brushed stray hairs away so he could gaze into the blue eyes. Not wanting to startle her, but knowing she'd listen to his warning, he said, "Jessie, Turley said he's looking for a gunslinger, promise me you won't leave the house."

Her body began to tremble. "A gunslinger?" Fear stole the shine from her eyes.

"I won't let anyone hurt you." His thumb glided over soft skin, tracing her cheek bone and wishing he could take away the fear. "Don't worry."

"A gunslinger in Dodge was after Russell," she said. The arms around his waist tightened. "He was scary and mean."

"You're safe here. I only wanted you to know so you'd stay inside for the next few days. If you must go outside, be sure Sammy is with you."

At the sound of his name, the dog tried to press his head between their knees. Jessie looked down. Kid took a step back, giving the dog room to rub his big head against her skirt. Her fingertips dug into his waist, not letting him step further away.

"Are you leaving again?" she asked.

"No, I'll be here the rest of the day. I'm just going to go unsaddle Jack."

"Can I come with you?" Her face scrunched up, blue eyes pleaded.

At any time during the past few days, he could have taken her, made her his wife in every way. And Lord knows he wanted to. These extra liberties he'd allowed himself since his return from Dodge were not satisfying enough. Oh, in some ways they were, but in other ways they simply made him want more. Every smile, touch, and kiss made him desire her more. He'd never known how bad unfulfilled needs could hurt. Somehow Jessie had weaved her way into his heart, making him love her beyond belief.

He smiled and tickled her chin, encouraging a small grin to lift the corners of her lips. "Yes, if you want to."

Her smile broadened. "Come on, Sammy," she said as they stepped toward the door, one of his arms still around her shoulders, one of hers around his waist.

It wasn't hard loving her. The hard part would be letting her go. Very soon he'd have to put her on the train for Boston. He'd almost forgotten about his plan. But like Satan knocking on hell's door, Turley had brought a telegram the Women's University sent to Dodge. Adam had forwarded it to Nixon. The school had an opening.

He'd done some quick figuring and between tuition, board and room, and train fares, it would only cost him fifteen hundred dollars. Almost three times as much as he'd expected, but he didn't have a choice. Jessie was family and a man took care of his family.

Kid let his hand slip from her arm to her waist as they walked down the porch stairs. It would mean he couldn't buy cattle for sometime, and would have to sell quite a few, but somehow he'd make it happen. Damn, he was going to miss her, but she would be safe at the school. Away from Montgomery, away from Russell, and away from him-though he'd never intentionally do her bodily harm, her virtue was no longer safe. He could now understand what it meant to be a rutting boar.

Not happy Turley knew more about his personal business than necessary, but unwilling to leave Jessie alone while he made the ride to Nixon himself, he'd asked the sheriff to send another message to the college- this one asking when she should arrive.

****

A week later Jessie, more frustrated than she'd ever been in her life, slammed the back door shut. Her body trembling, knees weak, she stumbled to the table and plopped onto a chair.

"I just want to scream, Sammy!"

Cautiously, the dog eased to her side, his nose

sniffing her skirt before he laid his head across her knees.

Stroking his glossy hair, she sighed. "I'm not mad at you. I'm not even mad at Kid. I'm mad at me. I just don't understand."

It wasn't the fact she'd begun to feel cooped up, not allowed to leave the safety of the house. Nor that Kid was forever under foot, she could barely turn around without bumping into him. That much she enjoyed, even relished. It was the fact that from everything she'd read, by now Kid should have taken her to his bed, made her his wife in everyway. After all, they were married and that's what happened in each of the stories. She'd read the romance novels so many time the pages were limp from use.

The kiss they shared on the back porch moments ago left a hot, burning need in the lowest region of her torso. She didn't know what to do about it, nor what to do to make Kid consummate their marriage.

Her cheeks burned as she recalled her latest attempt. She'd gotten the idea from one of the stories. Last night she'd "accidentally" left her robe in her room, so after bathing, she had nothing but a thin towel wrapped around her body. She'd paused in the living room where Kid sat near the fire place, reading a book, to apologize for her attire before walking up the steps.

But it hadn't work. He hadn't followed her up the stairs, as the man in the book had done. Instead, a look of pain or anger crossed his face before he went back to reading, and told her to run on up and get dressed for bed before she caught a cold.

She laid her head on the table, squeezing her lids shut against stinging tears. A knock on the door made her quickly wipe at her eyes, before she turned to the sound of someone entering.

With a wide smile, Bug walked in. "Hi, Jessie."

"Hi, Bug. How are you today?" she enquired, trying to sound friendly.

"Fine. How are you?"

"I'm good," she lied.

"Kid around? He wanted me to drop this off." He held out a tapestry bag.

She frowned. "He just went out to the barn. Did you check there?"

"Nope." Bug walked over and set the bag on the table. "Have you made any more of those molasses cookies? Ma says those type of treats should only be made at Christmas time."

"Really?" She stood, walked to the counter, and removed the cloth from a plateful of cookies. "Hog never told me that, and Kid really likes them." She set the plate on the table near where he'd sat.

"So do I." Bug took two, popping one in his mouth as the back door opened again.

"Hi, Kid," he mumbled around the cookie, and after swallowing added, "I brought the traveling bag you wanted."

Kid stood in the doorway, an odd frown on his face as his gaze settled on the bag. He glanced from it to her. His questioning look made her peer at the luggage. An eerie feeling caused the hair on her neck to stand up. He walked across the room, gave her elbow a soft squeeze before he took a cookie from the plate.

"Thanks, Bug. Have a minute to come out to the barn with me?"

"Sure." Bug took two more cookies before he rose and walked toward the door.

Kid took a bite of the cookie, gave her one of his heart melting smiles, and followed the younger brother outside. When the door snapped shut, Jessie picked up the bag, unbuttoned the flap and stared into the empty satchel. Setting it back on the table, she rubbed at the goose bumps popping out on her forearms. What would Kid need a traveling bag for?

Sammy whimpered, sticking a cold nose against her elbow. She knelt down, wrapped her arms around the dog's neck, and whispered, "Where ever he's going, hopefully he won't need to be gone long."

The dog tolerated her hard hug for an extended length of time, absorbing some of her sadness, before he began to wiggle and tug out of her hold.

"Sorry," she giggled, feeling apologetic for confining the animal. Taking a cookie from the plate, she handed it to him. "Here, you deserve a treat too."

Sammy ate it in one gulp, looking up for seconds before he'd even swallowed. She handed him one more then carried the plate to the counter before leaving the room to gather the laundry she planned to wash.

Later that day, after the laundry and supper dishes were clean, dry, and put away, she wandered into the living room to read. The evening sun flowed through the huge windows, casting a red hue across the room. The sight of Kid, sitting with his back to the glass, bathed in the sun's blaze took her breath away. A hand flew to her chest as wet, hot moisture bubbled in the pit of her body.

His gaze rose, locked onto hers. Fearing her legs would give out; she moved to the closest chair and collapsed in the soft seat.

"Are you all right?" Kid asked with furrowed brows.

"Yes, yes, fine, thank you." She fidgeted with the ruffles on her skirt, rearranged the way the rows had fallen around her knees, while secretly trying to bring her breathing under control.

Kid let out a long sigh and set the book on the table beside him. "Jessie, I have something to tell you."

"Oh?" She swallowed. Had he noticed the missing stories? Did he know she'd read them?

He rose, walked to the fireplace, and with his back to her, settled both hands on the mantle.

"Yes. I..." His shoulders lifted as he took another deep breath.

"What is it Kid? Has something happened?" *Russell!* She hadn't thought about him in several days, but had heard Joe had sent him to a line camp. The news had brought relief, knowing he was no where near her or Kid.

"Oh no. What has he done?"

Kid looked over his shoulder. "Who?"

"Russell," she sighed.

Kid twirled around searching the room with a fiery gaze. "Russell? Has he been here? When?"

"No, no he hasn't been here." She shook her head. "I haven't seen him."

"This isn't about Russell." Kid put his hands in his pant's pockets.

"It isn't?" The stories- it had to be the stories.

The toe of his left boot kicked at the rug on the floor, flipping the corner up then catching it as it flapped back down. After a few minutes he sighed and said, "Jessie, I've enrolled you in The Women's University."

Thank goodness it wasn't about the stories. Her shoulders eased with relief before she frowned, and asked, "The Women's University? I've never heard of that. What is it?"

"It's a school for women located outside Boston." His gaze landed on her. "You'll be leaving in the morning."

Dead air stung her lungs. Her body trembled. "L-leaving?" It wasn't new, she'd been asked or forced to leave every place she'd ever lived, but this time, the news scorched her heart like a hot iron.

"What have I done wrong?"

"Wrong?" Kid stepped closer. "You haven't done anything wrong."

She looked at him, not believing his words.

"Trust me, sweetheart, you didn't do anything wrong. It's just- well, it's the best thing for you. It's a woman's school, Jessie. You'll enjoy it."

"But I don't want to leave." Jessie pressed a hand to her lips, realizing she'd said her thoughts aloud. She blinked, trying to hold the tears in.

Kid knelt down in front of her. "You'll feel differently once you get there. You'll soon make friends with girls from all across the country."

"But who'll take care of you?" She wiped at the tears on her cheek. "Who'll cook and do the laundry?"

"I will."

"You will?" Her mind was spinning, not stopping long enough for full thoughts to form.

"Yes, I did it before, I can do it again."

She nodded, wiping again at the water on her face. "But-but who will take care of Sammy?"

"I will." Kid said. One of his thumbs rose to wipe at the tears still falling. "Don't cry now, Jessie. It's a fine place. You'll see." He took her hand, pulling her to her feet.

"Now you best run upstairs and pack. I put the traveling bag from Bug in your room. Use that for the train ride and pack your other things in one of the trunks."

A thick haze clouded her vision, and her body felt numb. Kid, one hand holding her elbow, the other in the middle of her back, pushed her forward and helped her manage the steps. In her bedroom, he released her.

"Let me know if you need any help."

She nodded, but he'd already shut the door, leaving her to pack. She crumbled to the floor and let the tears fall freely. It was several minutes before she wiped her eyes, and pulled a handkerchief from her skirt's hidden pocket near her waist. Blowing her nose into the dainty, lacy cloth, made the tears come again. It was the first hanky she'd ever owned. And why was she forever crying? She'd never cried before, but since coming to live here, she was forever doing so. It was like Kid and his kindness had opened every pent up feeling in her body. She pressed the cloth to her face and let the tears roll again.

Head throbbing and knees weaker than a newborn calf, Kid grabbed the banister to keep from falling down the flight of stairs. Sniffles and smothered sobs drifted through the wood of her bedroom door. Though barely audible, her crying pierced his ears as if it was louder than the train whistle in Dodge. Each muffled sound made his chest burn. A low whine rang out above the rest. He turned. Sammy, lying near her door, raised a paw and let his long claws trail down the wood.

Kid slapped his thigh. The dog ignored him.

He took a step, thumped the lab on the head and pointed to the stairs. Clearly disgusted, Sammy rose and without looking at Kid, plodded down the steps. He followed- his steps slow and unsteady.

Damn it to hell! He knew telling her was going to be hard, but he hadn't expected it to be this severe. If he were an animal, he'd head out to the back forty to lie down and die. When the bottom step loomed before him, he sat and pressed his face into the palms of his hands. Sharp stings burnt the backs of his eyes, and his throat felt as if it were on fire. Sending her away was the right thing to do. The only thing he could do.

He should have told her before now, gave her time to get used to the idea, but he couldn't. Fear that she'd persuade him to change his mind had made him keep silent. And then there were his desires. The real reason he'd refused to allow the thought of her leaving to enter his mind. When he saw the bag this afternoon, he'd wanted to throw up.

Carrying it up to her room after Bug left, he thought about throwing it out the window. He'd also thought about telling her then, but even a few hours could prove disastrous. Part of him had even thought about waiting until morning to tell her. But decided that wouldn't do. She needed a small amount of time. And he could make it though the night. Wouldn't crack under pressure and take her to bed, where there would be no turning back.

He wanted her, wanted her more than anything he'd ever wanted. More than becoming a rancher, more than building a fancy house, more than living, but that wasn't fair to her. She deserved to know there was more to life than what western Kansas had to offer. To know she could become anything she wanted to be.

He ran his hands through his hair. What if she did find the life she wanted and it didn't include him? A glob of pain bubbled up, into his throat where it attempted to choke him. Covering his mouth, he rose.

Sammy whined from near the front door. Kid walked across the room, opened the door, and followed the dog into the dark night. A mournful howl echoed off the porch roof. Kid didn't know if it came from him or Sammy. Unable to move any further, he grabbed the arm of a chair and collapsed onto it. Staring into the star-filled sky, he tried to get his body back under control, and convince himself if she found a life that didn't include him; he'd have to let her have it. It wouldn't kill him. Might paralyze him, but it wouldn't kill him.

****

When her crying bout played out, drained and hurting, Jessie blew her nose again, rose to her feet and walked to the bed. The carpet bag sat at the edge, waiting to be filled. She didn't even know how to pack. She'd only done it once, when she and Russell joined the wagon train leaving Independence years ago. That time she'd only been allowed one bag. Since then each time she'd been told to leave, her exits had been fairly instantaneous, which hadn't ever really mattered, since she'd never had anything to pack.

She sat down, the edge of the bed softly absorbing her weight. Not like this time. This time she had clothes, hair ribbons, feminine undergarments, and accessories, even a few knick knacks the brothers had given her. A robin egg from Bug, a carved dog from Snake, the small, glass vase Skeeter had brought her full of flowers. Jessie rubbed at her temples before she pushed off the bed. Shaky legs walked across the room to the dresser where the items sat. She touched each one. Grasping the carving with trembling fingers, her heart stung. How could she leave Sammy? And what would she do about all of Hog's recipes?

Still clutching the wood toy, she turned to the door. She couldn't leave, there was too much to do here. Something trickled into her spine and gave her strength, making her legs grow steady and firm. She tossed the toy onto the bed. That's all there was to it, she had too much to do.

She walked out of the room and down the stairs. The living room was empty, she moved to the open front door. Kid sat on the porch. Sammy left his side to greet her with one of his big grins. A slight weakness made her knees quiver, but she ignored it and stepped onto the porch.

"Do you need help?" Kid asked.

She took a deep breath and as her fingers clutched onto the material of her skirt said, "I've made a choice. I'm not leaving."

Kid's eyebrows rose, his mouth opened then closed as he ran a finger over his upper lip. A few quiet seconds hung in the air.

"Jessie, it's not your choice not to go."

"What do you mean? You said everyone always has a choice. And I'm choosing not to go." She crossed her arms, rubbed at chilled flesh, and hoped her courage wouldn't dissolve completely.

Kid rose. "Let's go back inside." His hand took her elbow, and he escorted her into the house.

Sammy bounded ahead, and then waited for her to sit before deciding where he wanted to lie down. Kid propelled her to one of the high back chairs, and the dog quickly settled near her feet.

"You do remember telling me that, don't you?" she asked as he moved away from the chair.

"Yes, Jessie. And you do have a choice. But it's not whether or not to go to Boston. Your choice is how you decide to react to the event. You have a choice to enjoy it and have fun, or to hate it and be miserable."

"That's not much of a choice."

"Nonetheless, it's your choice," he said. "Either way you will be attending the woman's college. Hog and Snake will be here early in the morning to take you to Dodge. You'll take the train from there to Boston."

"Why, Kid? Why do I have to go to Boston? Can't I learn everything here they could teach me there? If you buy the books I'll read them from cover to cover." She rose, stepped over Sammy, and grabbed his forearms, clutching the solid limbs.

"Please don't send me away Kid. I'll do anything you ask. Just please, please don't send me away," she begged, baring her greatest fear. The tears stung her eyes again, blurring his face.

He wrapped his arms around her and ran his fingers through the length of her hair. She buried her face to his chest, her heart breaking at the thought of leaving him.

Soft, cooing words filled her ears, calming her trembles and easing the cascade of tears. "Shh. Don't cry, Jessie." He kissed the top of her head. "I know it's hard. I don't want you to go either."

"Then why? Why are you sending me away?"

He pushed on her shoulders, separating them so he could look at her face. "I'm not sending you away because I want to. You're going to Boston because it's the best thing for you. You have your whole life ahead of you. At the college you'll learn new things, make new dreams. Figure out what you want to do with your life."

"But I already know what I want to do. I want to stay here." Didn't he understand that?

He let out a long, heavy sigh. "Right now that's what you want, but it's only because you haven't had many experiences to figure out what else is out there."

"Oh, yes I have, Kid. You wouldn't even believe all the things I've seen. All the things I've done." Her cheeks burned, remembering the few times she'd stolen food when every other attempts to gain some honestly had failed. She still feared someone would find out she stole.

"Jessie, there's a whole world out there you know nothing about." He made a slight grimace. "After three years in Boston you probably won't want to ever come back to Kansas."

Fear snaked up her body like a sidewinder, covering every nook and cranny. "Kid, I'll always want to come back here."

His arms pulled her forward, back into his solid, tight embrace. "And you'll always be welcome here, my sweet, sweet, Jessie."

She sighed at the closeness. Savoring the place she'd always yearn to be. It was sometime before his hold lessened, giving her room to tilt her head and look at his face. By then her mind had formed another question.

"Kid, when I come back...when I come back in three years, will I still be your wife?"

His dark eyes searched her face, pausing here and there. The tip of his finger, rough and soft at the same time, ran along the side of her cheek. It was a long time before he sighed, and said, "We'll talk about that in three years."

Her shoulders slumped, making her feel like a wilted flower. Russell had been right. Kid didn't want her as a wife, she wasn't good enough. But she'd been right too, Kid was a good man, he wouldn't send her back to the soddy. She stepped out of his embrace. No, he wouldn't kick her out, but he would send her to Boston, he'd send her as far away from him as possible.

"Be a good girl now, and go pack," Kid said as he turned his back to her.

****

Shoulders back, chest forward, and clutching the hateful bag, Jessie walked down the front steps as Hog and Snake loaded her trunk in the back of the wagon. Sammy, sensing something was wrong, ran around her ankles, almost tripping her. Each step was more painful than the last, but she gritted her teeth and kept moving.

A shiver ran up her spine as she heard Kid's voice.

"Bug!" he shouted from his stance near the wagon. "Grab Sammy and tie him to the porch."

Bug looked nervous as he crouched down and tried to coax Sammy to come to his side. The dog wouldn't have anything to do with the brother.

Fighting the breaking of her heart, Jessie patted her thigh then walked over to Bug. She knelt down, and wrapping her arms around Sammy, hugged him close as Bug tied the rope around his neck. Burying her face in the dark, silky hair, she kissed the tops of his wide ears before she stood and forced her legs to move to the wagon.

Kid stepped forward, meeting her near a back wheel. As he took the bag from her, she placed a hand on the edge of the wagon, balancing her wobbly stance. Sammy, no longer able to reach her, started barking and tugging at the rope. The noise made a new slice in her chest.

Kid took her elbow and led her near the wagon seat where he wrapped her in a hug. After a few moments, his hands framed her face.

"Don't be mad at me, Jessie."

The sob in the back of her throat came forward. Pressing her hands over her eyes, she shook her head. She could never be mad at him, she loved him too much.

His lips settled on her forehead, lingering there until she was ready to cry aloud. Then he lifted her into the wagon, his fingers slipping away as his normally rough voice, softly whispered, "Good-bye, Jessie."

Sammy's barks increased. She pressed her fingers against her eyelids, forcing the tears to stay put. Hog took a hold of the reins and the bench seat sagged as Snake crawled up on her other side. The wagon jolted forward and the wheels began to turn. Unimaginable pain formed tight knots in her body.

"Bye, Jessie!" Bug's voice rang out above the barking.

She gasped for air and turned around, blinking and trying to focus. Bug waved a hand high in the air. Kid stood beside him, hands behind his back. Sammy, stretching the rope as far as he could, yipped and howled at the departing wagon. He pawed at the air, then backed up and leaped forward. The rope went tight, slamming him back onto the ground with a loud yelp. Tears and sobs burst from their holds at the same time.

Snake reached out, one arm meant to wrap around her in comfort. She pushed it away. Nothing could ease the pain ripping across her chest.

Kid witnessed her refusal to be calmed as the wagon roll away. Pain seared his heart like a hot branding iron. The rattle of the wheels could barely be heard over Sammy's barking and howling. The dog jumped, twisted, and bit at the rope, doing his damnedest to follow his mistress. Kid knew just how he felt. Sending Jessie away was by far the hardest thing he'd ever done. It just might break him. Sweat popped out on his forehead.

"Jessie sure looked sad, didn't she, Kid?" Bug said with cheerless eyes.

Kid swallowed, making sure his voice wouldn't crack when he spoke, "Yes, Bug, she looked sad."

"I sure am going to miss her."

He patted the boy's back. His hand shook. He balled it into a fist and let it fall to his side. "So am I, Bug, so am I." The wagon turned, following the road around the calving pens. Kid wiped at the sting in his eyes as the travelers disappeared.

"You leaving now, too?" Bug asked.

Chapter Eleven

"In a few minutes, let them get a head start on us." Kid turned to Sammy. The dog had his nose pointed straight up, a long, mournful howl-song rose into the forlorn quiet. The tune was more ear-piercing and sadder than any coyote ever sang. It made his spine quiver.

"Sammy!"

Startled the dog stopped the howl mid-note and lowered his head. Slowly, he swung the wide neck around, curled his front lip, and gave a low, hateful growl.

Pissed at the world, Kid scowled back at the dog. "Oh, shut up!"

He turned to Bug. "Don't untie him."

"I won't, Kid. I won't!" Bug shook his head.

Joe led two horses to the front porch. The saddle bags bulged. "You ready?"

"Yeah, I don't want them to be too far ahead of us." Kid mounted Jack, flipped the horse around and said, "We'll be back in a couple days, as soon as we make sure Jessie and the boys get to Dodge safely."

"All right, Kid." Bug gave a nervous look toward Sammy.

The dog stared straight ahead, watching the road, waiting for Jessie to return. He didn't even bat an eye toward him and Joe as they rode out. "Traitor," Kid mumbled.

Another low growl filled the air behind him.

"Even your dog's mad at you over this one," Joe said as he rode beside him.

Kid sent a disgusted stare toward the other man.

"Hey, I didn't say I was mad, said the dog was."

"Will you shut up?" He didn't want to hear it right now. His head throbbed, his guts were raw, hell, his whole body ached. The last thing he wanted was some chatterbox riding beside him all the way to Dodge.

"He's probably just wondering why you gotta send her all the way to Boston," Joe added.

"Because that's the only place she'll be safe." He had tried to come up with another plan, barely sleeping a wink all night. Several times he'd come close to entering her room, telling her she didn't have to leave, telling her he couldn't let her leave. But he hadn't, nor had another plan formed.

"Hell, I thought she was pretty safe at the ranch. That house you built is stronger than Fort Dodge, and between the hands, your brothers, you, and me; Montgomery wouldn't ever get a chance at her. Her brother either for that matter. Skeeter's got him out in the middle of nowhere. You know, I almost feel sorry for the sap. A month with Skeeter...I couldn't do it."

"It's for Jessie too, you know. She deserves a chance to see what life has to offer besides this God forsaken land," Kid mumbled. Hoping someday he could believe his reasoning.

"I thought you loved this country."

"I do, but that doesn't mean everyone else does." He took his hat off and wiped his forehead with his arm.

Joe looked around, nodding his head. "I do."

Far ahead, little more than a dark blob on the barren land, he could make out the wagon that carried Jessie away. Would she ever want to come back? Would Boston and the Women's College change her so much she'd never want to see the rolling fields of the prairie again? He hoped not- no, he prayed not.

"Keep your eyes peeled for any movement, no one's seen Montgomery for several days," he said and spurred Jack into a canter. He wanted a moment to himself, a moment to mourn the loss of a love he never thought he'd experience.

****

The next afternoon, they boarded the train. Numb, somewhat scared, but newly determined Jessie smiled at the conductor as Hog carried her bag down the long isle and Snake handed their tickets to the man. The brothers were to travel all the way to Boston with her. She sincerely hoped Kid wouldn't be too mad at them when they told him what she'd done, but she couldn't include them in her plan. Besides, Kid was just like Sammy, all bark and no bite.

The long, dusty trail from the Triple Bar to Dodge had given her plenty of time to think, learn, and plan. Snake and Hog were quiet boys, unless you got them talking, then they couldn't be shut up. Her head still spun from everything they'd said. Kid did have a trip to Europe paid for, and it was a trip to find a wife.

The brothers said he'd been planning it since he was ten, when his father brought him to Kansas from Missouri and they'd stopped along the way at Sam Wharton's place. Kid laid a plan to become just like the rich rancher, which included traveling to Europe and bringing back a refined, well-bred woman to be his wife. The boys also assured her Kid always does what he plans.

Well, that was fine with her; she didn't want to be his wife. She didn't need him, her brother, or any other man telling her what to do. And she certainly didn't need to be sent across the nation. *Boston of all places!* If he didn't want her at the ranch, all he had to do was say so. She had her soddy.

She gritted her teeth, trying to appease the anger boiling in her stomach. It wouldn't be good for the boys to know how mad she was, they might suspect something. With one hand pressed against her stomach, she gave both Snake and Hog slight smiles as they sat down on the opposite bench.

Hog pushed her bag beneath his seat. A sense of longing rumbled through her veins, she'd miss the extra set of clothing, but it couldn't be helped, the bag might hamper her escape. She'd never jumped from a train, but figured both hands would be needed when the time came.

"Jessie, your stomach hurtin'?" Hog asked, clearly concerned.

"Hmm? Oh, yes a little, nerves I guess." She wasn't lying, her stomach did hurt. And she was as nervous as hell.

"There's nothing to be scared about. We're with you." Snake gave her a charming smile.

"I know." A loud whistle sounded. As it faded she added, "Thanks, you boys have really been good to me."

"Well, you're our sister. We gotta be good to you, or Ma would skin us alive," Hog said, giving her a wink.

"And Kid would kill us if'n something happened to you," Snake added, his tone serious.

"Kid won't kill you," she assured.

The boys glanced at each other, both silently saying they didn't believe her.

"He's not nearly as mean as he has you boys believing. Neither is Sammy."

They still didn't believe her.

The whistle sounded again, this time followed by

a hiss of steam. It was almost time to set her plan in motion. She took a deep, fortifying breath and let it settle in her chest. "I'm going to use the lavatory before we start to roll," she said, rising to her feet.

"Uh?" Snake asked.

"The privy," she whispered.

"Oh, all right," Hog replied.

Jessie walked between the rows of seats, to the back of the train car and two small closets. Lifting a latch, she glanced back to the boys. The smiles they returned tugged at her heart. She ducked into the little room, blinking at the sting in her eyes. Holding the door closed, she braced her feet, waiting for a jolt as the train whistle sounded one last time. A moment later it came. The car shook as large iron wheels began to turn. *There's still time to change your mind.* She ignored the thought, blew the air from her lungs, and opened the door a bit.

Peeking out the crack, she waited for the conductor to step up from the back platform. After he walked past the closet, she pushed the door a smidgen wider, and once assured the coast was clear, snuck out. Her feet nervously scampered through the boarding door and onto the platform.

The hitch between the passenger car and the box car attached to it clanked, the loud noise sent her heart to her throat. Hugging the outside wall, she fought to keep her balance and edged to the side, glancing each way. A sigh emitted, thankfully no one was about. Slowly, the train picked up speed, the ground began flowing beneath the metal platform like a river of sand and gravel.

The cattle pens beside the tracks filled the air with a foul, strong odor. Jessie tried to breathe beyond the smell, ducked beneath the wide safety rail, and pulled her body up on the other side. Positioning her toes on the thin edge of the platform frame, she clutched the safety bar behind her back and watched fence posts roll past.

At least Kid and Sammy had a bark, she didn't even have that. All she had were visions. Often she thought about wringing Russell's neck, or refusing to move again when one of his schemes had gone bad. But those visions had remained silent. She'd never acted on one....until this very moment.

The train moved fast enough now. If, by chance, someone saw her, the engine wouldn't be able to stop before she got away. She closed her eyes, took a deep breath, and jumped. Wind tousled her hair and skirt as she floated through the air.

Tucking her body into a ball moments before hitting the ground, she rolled across the rocks and into the grass. Disregarding the pain in her shoulder and hip, she quickly scrambled to her feet and ran between two of the foul smelling pens.

Stinky, slippery mud stuck to the soles of her shoes, she lifted the ends of the pink dress and trudged forward. Cattle mooed and scurried away from the fence rails as she ran past. Fearing watchful eyes, she kept her head low and weaved between the pens, the whole while praying she wouldn't heave from the smells. If she could get to one of the feed pens, she could hide out amongst the stacks of hay until nightfall. The frilly, pink dress, one of her favorites, was much too fancy to walk through the tent city on the south side of Dodge in the middle of the day.

Three pens later, she crawled beneath the fence railings and scampered into the middle. Squeezing between the huge stacks, she found a cavern, plenty large enough for her to hide. Jessie snuggled down, waiting for the rapid beating of her chest to slow, and listened for shouts she prayed wouldn't come.

****

Not until millions of twinkling stars decorated the black sky did she emerge and silently slip passed the cattle to find the well-worn trek to the tents. Fingers crossed, she skirted around hundreds of canvas shapes, looking for a familiar one. Coming upon four large barrels turned upside down, Jessie let out a thankful breath of air.

"Willamina?" she whispered near the long slit used as a door.

The light inside the canvas flickered then moved closer to the opening. "Jessica? Jessica is that you girl?" The material flipped outwards.

"Yes, it's me."

"Well, land sakes child! Get yourself in here!" Willamina waved an arm.

Jessie, very thankful to see the welcoming face of her old friend, stepped into the tent and into the embrace of the woman's gnarled hands. Tears threatened, but she bucked up, and forced her eyes to remain dry.

Willamina's face took on more wrinkles as she stepped back saying, "Land sakes, girl, what you been doing? Living with cows? You smell to high heaven!"

A true smile formed. "I'm afraid I chose the wrong pens to walk through."

"Take those shoes off, let me swish them out." Willamina's gaze started at her shoes and ended where the pink bow tied her long hair away from her face. "Goodness, girl, I ain't never seen anyone prettier than you. Why, you look like one of those gals in those picture books."

Jessie sat down, catching her balance as the rickety chair wiggled and began to untie her shoes. "I was afraid you may have moved on."

"Naw, too late in the year. I'll winter here." The woman took the shoes as Jessie removed them. "That no good brother with ya?"

"No, I really don't know where Russell is."

"Good. Good riddens to him. You got a dress, the

one you left behind, in that trunk over there." Williamia nodded toward a square box on the other side of the tent. "Dowse the light and put it on while I rinse these off, then I'll air out that fancy one. Got some men's clothes hanging by the creek I can hide it with, but we'll have to bring it in 'afore daylight."

Jessie nodded and rose to walk to the box.

"Then you can tell me where you got the fancy clothes and these new shoes." Willamina's friendly eyes grew cold. "Jessica, you're still a good girl, ain't ya?"

Jessie swallowed, wondering for a moment if some of the thoughts she'd had back at the ranch would count.

"Yes, Willamina, I'm still a good girl."

"Good, I can't be having bad girls living here." The woman turned to slip out the tent. "Dowse the light and change."

She did as instructed. As the old dress fell over her shoulders, she covered her face with both hands, missing the ranch and Kid with all her heart.

Early the following morning, wearing the worn thin dress of her past, but with the pink one wrapped in an old sack, Jessie climbed into the back of a wagon. The wood was grey, not the fresh, new brown of the one she'd traveled in to Dodge. Ignoring the remembrance, she waved good-bye to Willamina then hid her body amongst the cargo, where she'd stay until clear of the city and other travelers.

The trip to the soddy took two days, the wagon needing several hasty repairs along the way, but the family she traveled with were kind and happy. They were on their way to the state line, planned on homesteading across the Colorado border, where they had family waiting. The well-worn wagon trail ran west several miles north of her land. Jessie insisted the family not detour to take her any closer, assuring the walk wasn't a long one.

Full of benevolence, the Jackson's insisted she spend one last night with them and early the next morning, after feeding her breakfast and insisting she take a small bag of supplies, Bryce, Madeline, and their two year old son, Miles, headed west while Jessie began walking south.

It wasn't a long walk, but a lonely one. High in the sky, the sun beat on her shoulders as she topped the small hill behind the soddy. The little house, showing no sign of life, sat below- waiting for her. Jessie took a deep sigh.

She was home.

Sadder yet, she was alone. In this big, wide world, full of people, she was completely alone. It was a first; always in the past when she found a place to stay she'd had a glimmer of hope Russell would be happy with her find and that together they would begin to carve out a new life. This time she didn't even have that glimmer.

The wind, whipping at her skirts like the devil himself, pushed her forward. As her feet began to stumble down the hill, words floated through her mind. *"You have a choice, Jessie. We all do."*

Her toes dug in the sandy soil, and she twisted from side to side, looking to see if the words had only been in her head. Grassland, miles and miles of grassland, like an ocean of light brown, flowed beneath the bright blue sky. A few trees, a rock or two jutted up here or there, but nothing else. Kid was nowhere in sight.

She straightened her shoulders. "Him and his stupid choices!"

She began to stomp down the hill. "You have a choice, Jessie. No, that's not your choice, Jessie, this is." The sound of her voice sent a prairie chicken, wings a flutter, to run across her path as she made her way to the sod shanty. By the time she stood in front of the thick, wood door, she had made a choice.

Or maybe it was a conclusion. Either way, Kid Quinter was a vile man, and she hated him, hoped she'd never see him ever again.

****

Kid set the bowl on the floor of the front porch. "Come on, Sammy. You at least have to drink some water."

The dog lifted the corner of his upper lip, showing one yellow fang as he emitted a heartless growl.

"I'm not afraid of you, so you can quit acting." Kid reached a hand forward.

Sammy snapped at the fingers.

Kid pulled his hand back, frowning. "Fine, be that way."

Closing his eyes, Sammy repositioned his head on his front paws, his sides heaving with a big sigh.

A faint sound, the clatter of a wagon made Kid stand up to scan the road. Sammy, on the other hand, didn't even bat an eyelid. Kid hated the thought of putting the dog down, but the poor thing was starving itself to death. With the toe of his boot, he pushed the bowl closer to the long, black snout then moved to the steps, walking down as a buckboard rounded the calving pens.

Squinting against the sun, he blinked several times, questioning the sight. His steps quickened. Grabbing the leather straps of one harness while the horse jolted to a stop, Kid asked, "What the hell are you two doing here?"

"Well, uh, now Kid, that's kind of a funny story-" Snake started.

"I'm not finding anything funny! You two should be in Boston about now." The harness slipped from his hand as he ran to the wagon bed. A large, carved trunk and a dusty traveling bag sat on the floorboards.

"Where the hell is Jessie?" he shouted passed

the lump in his throat. His heart pounded so hard he could hear it in his ears.

Something solid hit his arm as a black flash leaped into the bed. Sammy began sniffing at the cargo, whining, his fat tail whipping back and forth before Kid's face. Kid reached up, grabbed Snake by the front of the shirt and pulled him to the ground. His bottom jaw tight, teeth clenched so hard he could barely speak, he growled, "Where the hell is she?"

Fingers tried to pull his hands from the material. They did little more than make his grasp tighten. "Kid? Kid, let go of Snake, and I'll tell you what happened." Hog's grunting voice sounded near his ear.

Kid let go of Snake, but only with one hand so he could use it to grab Hog's shirt collar.

"Where the hell is she?"

Hog swallowed, his Adam's apple catching on the material. "Well, um, uh, here?"

"Here?" Kid screeched. Cold sweat covered the back of his neck.

The brothers nodded.

Kid let go, using his hands to press at the pain throbbing in his temples. He took a deep breath. Killing them wouldn't help. Then he'd never find out what happened. Placing his hands on his hips, he bent forward, sucking in gulps of air. The ground swirled before his eyes.

"Kid? Kid you all right?" Snake asked.

"No, I'm not all right," he said, still trying to calm his shaking body.

"You ain't dying or something, are ya?" Hog asked.

He flipped his head upright. "No, I'm not dying, but you two are. As soon as you tell me what happened. I'm going to have to kill you," he said, fully meaning the words.

The boys started backing away from him.

"Stop!" He pointed a finger at them. "Stop right there. Don't take another step until I get every detail."

Joe appeared beside him, looking between him and the brothers.

"What's up? Why are these two back?"

"They're just about to tell me that." His fists clenched. He folded his arms across his chest so he wouldn't wring their necks before they got the story out.

Joe ran a finger over his chin, and said, "What happened, Hog?"

"Well, we made it into Dodge, no problem," he started.

"None whatsoever," Snake added. "And we boarded the train."

"That much I know!" Kid took a step forward.

Joe's hand slapped down on his shoulder as the man said, "We followed you to Dodge, made sure you made it all right."

"You did?" Hog asked.

"Yes, and we watched both of you and Jessie board the train. What happened?" Kid asked. Pulsating blood pounded through his body, making every muscle tight. If the boys didn't talk faster, he would explode from the tension.

"Well, the train pulled away from the station and Jessie said she had to use the privy. When she didn't come back, we went to check on her, but she was gone. Just up and vanished," Hog said.

Snaked nodded. "We looked everywhere, even had the conductor helping us. When we got to Abilene we checked the other ca-"

"Abilene?" Kid interrupted. "You lost her in Dodge, but didn't stop the train until Abilene?" They were more incompetent than he thought.

"They wouldn't let us, Kid. We tried!" Hog took

another step backwards.

Joe's hand on his shoulder tightened. "Kid, they wouldn't have stopped the train for them. You know that." The hand patted. "Calm down a touch."

Through the red haze in front of his eyes, Joe's worried face formed. Kid ran a hand through his hair, pulling at the roots, hoping the pain might bring his fury back under control.

"We, uh, we got her trunk, turned in our tickets and caught the next train back to Dodge," Hog said.

"From there we took the stage to Nixon, got in last night, walked home and this morning went back to pick up her trunk and bring it out here," Snake finished the tale.

Kid choked on his own air. "You got in last night, but waited until this afternoon to tell me Jessie is missing?"

"W-we figured she'd already be here. Thought she'd want her belongings," Hog said.

"You mean she really ain't here?" Snake said, a worried frown covering his face.

"No, she's not here!" Kid shouted.

"Well, shit! Where is she?" Hog asked.

Snake nodded, looking at him expectantly, "Yeah, Kid, where is she?"

"How the hell am I supposed to know? You two were supposed to take her to Boston!" He flipped around, kicking at the dirt beneath his feet. Sammy sat in the wagon, his head resting on the top of the trunk with sad brown eyes watching his every movement. Kid snapped back around to the brothers.

"Did either of you think of sending a wire?"

They looked at each other, mouths agape, clearly having the thought of sending him a telegram for the very first time.

"Go saddle some horses." Kid pointed to the barn. "Including Jack."

"Why?" Hog asked.

"Because we're going to Dodge to look for her!"

"But Ma's expecting us for supper. If'n we don't show up, she'll be thinking you done killed us," Snake said.

"And I will, if you don't go saddle those horses." He hoisted a fist near his shoulder, turned and smashed it against the side of the wagon. "Go! Now!"

The boys scattered, running for the barn. Joe's hand landed on his shoulder again. "We'll find her."

"It's been ten days, Joe. Ten God-damned days since she rode away on that wagon." His eyes stung and his chest was aflame, both pains far stronger than the slight sting running across his knuckles.

"I know, but she couldn't have gone far." Joe turned, pointed toward the bunk house. "I'll go pack some grub and tell one of the ranch hands to take care of the wagon."

He nodded, waiting for the man to leave. Hoping he'd walk away before the water behind his eyes came forward. He never should have sent her away. It was his fault. He'd put her in danger. He squeezed his eyes against imagined visions of her. Injured, scared, and crying for help.

"We'll find her, Kid," Joe said.

The fury he'd felt at his brothers wasn't nearly as strong as the fear overtaking his body. He swallowed, forcing the log in his throat to roll over. "Yeah, but what if Montgomery already has?"

Chapter Twelve

The tents went on forever. Every shape and size, and not one of them fit for Jessie to live in. Kid reined Jack to a halt and turned to the three riders beside him. "Hinkle said Jessie used to live near a woman named Willamina Smith. She takes in laundry, so her tent will most likely have tubs and clothes hanging up around it. Snake, you and Hog go around that way, Joe you go along the center trail, I'll take the bottom half."

"What do we do when we find her?" Hog asked.

Kid glared, but before he said anything, Snake slapped the back of Hog's head and the two of them moved toward tent city.

Joe resettled in his saddle. "What else did the sheriff say?"

Kid sighed. "Not much. He hasn't seen Jessie, nor heard anything about her jumping the train, or being in town. He hasn't heard anything about Montgomery lately either." Sweat trickled down his back, and he arched at the quiver it caused.

"He said he's been busy with rustlers lately, wondered if we've had any trouble." Kid scratched the back of his head. He didn't have time to worry about some damn cows, not when Jessie was missing and some bastard was out looking for her. He nudged Jack forward.

In no time, he discovered every other tent had

tubs and clothes hanging beside them. Kid didn't bother to re-mount, just led Jack on to the next one, and the one after that.

The sun, deep in the western sky, blazed off a woman's crouched back near a larger tent as he and Jack continued their way through the haphazard city. Gray hair fell from the bun used to keep the stiff tendrils out of her face as she scrubbed something over a washboard.

His fingers began to tremble. Stopping a short distance away, Kid asked, "Willamina Smith?"

The woman's head snapped up, squinting green eyes glared at his face. "Who wants to know?"

Hope made his pulse increase.

"Excuse me for interrupting you, Ma'am, but I'm looking for someone."

The material fell into the water with a loud plop, but her curved spine didn't straighten as she turned and started to walk toward him. Using the front of her skirt to wipe her hands, she looked him from head to toe before saying, "You're him, ain't ya?"

Kid dropped Jack's rein and stepped forward, pulling a chair from beside the tent closer for her to rest her stooped body on. "Excuse me?"

The woman sat down, her head nodding. "You're Jessica's man. Ain't ya?"

Kid smiled, remembering she'd mentioned once that Jessie was her nickname.

"If you're referring to Jessie Johnson, then yes, she's who I'm looking for. Is she here?"

"You look just like I expected ya too. All tall, straight backed, mighty fine looking." She let out a little laugh, but then squinted blazing green eyes at him again and said, "Jessica's a good girl ya know."

"Yes, Ma'am, I know." Kid looked to the tent, wondering if it had moved. "Is she here?"

The woman shook her head. "Nope."

"Well, then, could you tell me where she is?"

Once more, the woman looked him up and down, her long pause made him hold his breath.

She tugged at a floppy ear lobe. "I suppose I could."

He let out the breath, feeling throttled. For a few minutes he liked Willamina Smith, thinking the old woman had a kind and generous soul, now he realized she held out for an offer of money. He dug in his pocket. Deep down he'd expected as much.

"How much?"

"How much?" She gave him a puzzled look.

Pulling out a wad of bills, he folded a few open. "How much for you to tell me where Jessie is?"

She laughed. A loud, giggling sound like she was tickled pink.

He handed her the wad. "Here, if this isn't enough, I'll get you more. I'm good for it."

She continued to laugh. "I'm sure you are." Her lips pulled together, stifling her giggles. "But, Sonny, even you ain't got enough money for me to tell you where Jessica is."

His cheek twitched with anger. He opened his mouth, but before a word came out Willamina held up her hand.

"You ain't got enough money, 'cause I'll tell you for free." She patted the bottom of an upside down tub, looking at him expectantly.

Anger oozed out, replaced with relief. He lowered, sitting on the bucket beside her.

"I have to find her, Willamina. She may be in danger."

"Montgomery?"

He nodded.

"He's a rotten soul."

"Yes, he is."

"But you're not. I can see it in your eyes. I can also see you love Jessica, just as I saw her love for you in her baby blues."

Kid squirmed, but as the woman's words settled, he straightened, accepting what she saw as the truth. Saying nothing, but warmed by the thought of Jessie's returned love, he nodded.

"I was in love once." She stared off in the distance. "We had a fine house, up by Abilene. Oh, nothing big, but a good solid soddy, and we were happy. Then Paul died. Snake bit. There were too many of them. The well had gone dry, and he was diggin' us a new one. Dug right into a rattler's den." She shook her head. "I had to leave then, with no water I couldn't keep our critters alive. Not even the chickens." She sighed.

He wrapped a hand around the red, rough one lying on her knee.

"You moved here after that?" Part of him wanted to scream, he needed to find Jessie. The other part told him to slow down, give the woman a moment, the few minutes she needed wouldn't matter.

"No, I lived in Abilene for years, until my sister asked me to come to Dodge. She was ailing and needed help." Willamina turned to him. "She died 'afore I arrived." Her other hand patted the top of his.

"The tent city was only about half the size it is now, and I realized there were plenty of young girls that needed me. They needed a mother to keep them good. Been here for five years now." A crooked smile covered her face. "But enough about me, you're needing to find your gal, ain't ya?"

Kid smiled back, nodded and said, "Yes, Ma'am." The wad of bills crinkled in his other hand. He loosened his hold, handing the money to her.

She smiled, but shook her head. "I don't want your money, Kid." One hand rose to pat his cheek. "Jessica told me your name. She told me a lot about you." The gnarled fingers pushed the hand holding the money away. "You keep your money, but promise me something, Kid."

He nodded. "Anything."

"Promise me you'll keep Jessica a good girl. Promise you won't let anyone ever hurt that young gal again. She doesn't deserve it."

"I promise, Willamina. I promise." It was an easy vow to make. He'd rather die than see Jessie hurt.

She pulled her other hand from beneath his. "Then get out of here. Go get your girl."

He rose, his heart pounding, ready to jump on Jack and fly to Jessie's side. His feet stalled as he stuttered, "Y-you haven't told me where she is yet."

"Well, hell's bells!" Willamina laughed. "And here I was thinking my back would give out 'afore my mind." Sparkling green eyes met his. "She's at her soddy."

Air swooshed from his lungs as if someone had punched him in the stomach. "Her soddy?" Not once had he thought of looking for her there.

"Yes! Now get out of here." Willamina waved one hand.

It was hard, but he made feet that wanted to run, walk to Jack. Her soddy- all this time she'd only been a few miles away.

"Hey, Kid? When you see Jessica, tell her Willamina say's hi."

He mounted the horse, and steering Jack near the chair where Willamina still sat, he tossed the wad of bills onto her lap.

"I will. And when you're ready to move out of this place, look up the Triple Bar Ranch." He gave her a wink. "We can always use a good wash woman."

Willamina's light giggle filtered the evening air as he spurred Jack and rode away from the tents.

Joe crossed his path before the horse had room

to leap into a gallop. "Hey, where you headed?" he asked.

"To get Jessie!" Kid steered around the man.

"Well, where is she?" Joe asked.

"Her soddy!" He shouted over his shoulder.

****

Jessie walked out of the sod house and into the bright morning sun. The rays sparkling down did little to brighten her mood. She stared overhead. Where was the gloom? Why couldn't the sky be gray and full of clouds, giving her clear reasons to feel so dreary? She bent, picked up a rock, and tossed it toward the tall grass beside the house. It fell short, with a loud thud it rolled against a thick board. One of the many Joe and the other hands had used to strengthen the structure of her small home.

The changes had surprised her when she first arrived. She'd forgotten he'd said he'd repair it. Solid wood planks covered all of the outer walls, and new shutters hung where old ones once sagged. A long sigh left her lungs. The improvements kept the snakes out, and they'd help keep the winter weather out as well. She should be happy, the men's good deeds meant she had more time for other chores, but nothing could lift the depressed shroud settled around her frame. At times she wondered how her heart continued to beat, something as broken as it should have stilled days ago.

Jessie shook her head, hoping the movement would send the thoughts away. She had more this fall than she'd had the past five- a good, solid place to stay warm as winter slipped closer. She should focus on finding provisions. Nuts, berries, even some meat she could dry for the winter months. The few supplies the Jackson's had given her were almost gone, she'd been lazy, using them instead of finding others. What was wrong with her? She'd never been so lax in her life. Slapping her palms against her thighs, she stepped forward, moving toward the small wind-row of trees behind the house. Perhaps there would be something in the snare she'd set last night.

The wind blew through the trees, knocking leaves from their branches. Flapping and fluttering they fell against her skirt. The dried and curled leaves didn't bother her, nothing did. She almost wished she could be like them, just curl up and blow away.

A noise caused her to pause and listen for the direction of which it came. If possible, her heart grew heavier. It was the snare. Moving forward again, she walked through the tall weeds to where she'd set the small trap. Jessie knelt down and separated the grass.

A little bunny, trembling with fear, backed into the corner of the stick pyramid as she leaned closer. Large enough to skin, she could make a week's worth of meals from the rabbit. Tiny, brown eyes tried to avoid contact with her. Her face scrunched and she lifted the trap.

"Don't fear, little one," she whispered. Paralyzed with fright, the bunny didn't move. Jessie ran a hand over the soft fur then pushed at his rump. "Go on, off with you. I'd rather have eggs any day."

The rabbit shot forward, quickly disappearing in the waving grass. Leaving the trap unset, she moved away, and made a half-hearted attempt to look through the weeds for a prairie chicken roost. Eggs were easy to eat- she didn't have to kill anything to have a meal. A rustle sounded. Believing it was the escaping bunny, she didn't turn around, choosing instead to continue her search.

The noise came again, louder and closer. She straightened and turned as a black glob leaped over the tall grass. An excited bark sliced the air as the animal flew toward her.

"Sammy?"

The dog hit her in the middle of the chest, knocking her down. Her bottom smacked the ground, making the air swoosh from her lungs. Sucking in a fresh breath, she flipped onto her knees and wrapped her arms around the head sniffing her up and down. "Sammy, oh, Sammy, I missed you so much."

He snuggled close, his body trembling as she laid her head against his soft, silky hide. For several minutes she relished his unexpected arrival before thoughts formed. Sammy? If Sammy was here, it meant one thing...Kid wasn't far behind.

Trembles started in her toes and rose to encompass every inch of her frame. Caused by fear or excitement, she didn't know. Wiping at the wetness under her eyes, she gave Sammy one more solid hug before she stood, turning to the eyes boring holes in her back.

The morning sun haloed the tall frame. One foot was settled on a fallen log, making a lean leg bend at the knee. A gun belt hung low on his hips, the holster strapped to his thigh with a leather lace. Narrow hips grew into a wide, solid chest, which was partially covered by the brawny arms folded across it. As usual the top button of his shirt was undone, allowing dark, curly hair to peek out. She bypassed the face, not wanting to see the anger in those dark, obsessive eyes. His head, tilted sideways a touch, was covered with the wide hat that sat cockeyed across his dark hair. All in all, it was the vision she saw every night in her dreams.

Lack of air made her considerably dizzy. She'd forgotten how to breathe. Opening her mouth, she hoped the air would flow in on its own. It did, making her cough.

The foot stepped off the log, straightening his stance as he moved forward. She held up a hand. He couldn't come any closer, if he did, she might lose her mind and run to his arms, begging for forgiveness.

Sammy nudged her knee. She placed a hand on his head, letting it run along his back, over his lean side, between his ribs. *Ribs!* Her eyes snapped at the man.

"Kid Quinter haven't you been feeding this dog?"

Kid stopped, a slow smile lifted the corners of his mouth.

Her heart somersaulted.

"He wouldn't eat."

She frowned and rubbed Sammy's ears. "Why not?"

"I suspect because he was missing you."

Her fingers once again felt the stiff bones and sunken stomach. "Well, you should have thought about that before you sent me away." Shocked at her outburst, Jessie slapped her other hand over her mouth.

Kid moved forward, a chuckle floating on the breeze. "Yes, I should have." He stopped in front of her. "I should have thought of a lot of things before I sent you away, Jessie."

Mere inches separated them. Heat from his body hovered, teasing her with his undeniable warmth. His heavenly, musky scent filled her nose. Unsticking her tongue from the roof of her mouth, she swallowed.

His hand came forward, the tips of his fingers brushed against her arm, renewing the uncontrollable trembles. Suddenly, her breasts crushed against his chest. Her nose pressed into the opening of his shirt and big, comforting hands roamed her back.

"Jessie, I'm sorry. I'm so very sorry."

The lips, softly kissing the top of her head, were her undoing. With a sob, she wrapped her arms around him, clutching, pressing every bit of her body against his. Her fingers searched his back, feeling every curve, every hard muscle as her torso drank heat from his sculpted chest.

"Oh, Kid. I thought I'd be happy here. I thought..."

"Shh, sweetheart, shh," he murmured, kissing her hair again.

The kisses moved downward, she lifted her face, treasuring each touch. Hot breath and wet lips floated over her forehead, across her cheeks, and finally against her mouth. Starving for his taste, she devoured his lips.

Her arms tightened, unable to get close enough, every muscle strained to merge them into one. His body, so hot, so perfect beneath her fingers drove her into a frenzy of passion. Minutes or hours may have slipped by; she had no way of knowing, too busy savoring every inch of her husband.

It wasn't until a loud rip vibrated the air that they separated. Startled, they both looked downward to where Sammy sat. A large chunk of Kid's shirt sleeve dangled from the dog's mouth.

"You damn dog," Kid said with a soft laugh.

The sound of his voice penetrated her mind. He was real; it wasn't one of her late night dreams. The realization made her giggle. The dog stood, and tail wagging, stuck his head against her thigh. She scratched his ears.

"That was naughty, Sammy."

Her reprehend didn't faze him, he snuggled closer, making room for him between she and Kid. The slight separation made more thoughts form. She bit her bottom lip and stared at the buttons on Kid's shirt.

"W-what are you doing here?"

He tilted her chin up. "I came to get you. Bring you back to the ranch."

She shook her head. "I-I can't..."

"You can't what?"

Jessie stepped away. She couldn't think straight with him so close.

"I-I can't go to Boston."

"Who said anything about Boston?" He stepped forward and ran a hand along her upper arm. "I said the ranch, Jessie."

His slightest touch made her shiver with longing. Since she had no pride left, she might as well bare her soul.

"Kid, I know I'm not the wife you want. I know I'm not from Europe and I'm not well-bred. I'm not smart, nor elegant." She glanced up, meeting his gaze. "But I'll do anything, everything I can to become a wife you can live with. I'll read every book, study until my eyes fall out, anything you want." Holding her head high, she proclaimed, "I love you, Kid."

He didn't move, just stood before her, mouth agape.

She took a deep breath and continued, "I've learned something the past two weeks. I've always known I can live without fancy clothes. I can live without bountiful food. I can even live without a house. But I learned I can't live without you." She shook her head, forcing herself not to choke as she admitted, "Without you, I just want to wither up and die."

His hand clutched her shoulder, dragging her back into his embrace.

"I can't live without you either, sweetheart." Wide, warm palms framed her face and gentle fingers wiped away her tears. "Without you, I want to wither and die, too."

She forgot to breathe again. "You do?"

He nodded. "And there's nothing you need to learn. I love you just as you are."

Air swooshed in and out of her lungs so fast she became light headed.

"You do?"

His lips came down. Sweet and intoxicating, they pressed against hers as he said, "I do."

****

A week later, more satisfied and content than he ever deemed possible, Kid pulled the alluring naked form of his wife closer, running a hand over skin so soft, he had to stroke it a second time to make sure it was real as she snuggled against him. The heat of their lovemaking left her body glistening with tiny beads of sweat. He pulled the covers up to cocoon her, not wanting even a chill to touch her.

Smooth fingertips stroked his chest, leaving a hot trail, and moist lips pressed against his neck before teeth nipped at the skin, providing nothing close to pain.

"Kid?" she asked.

"Hmm?"

"Are you happy?"

"Extremely," he answered truthfully. One hand went up to fondle the long locks flowing over her shoulders.

"You?"

She nodded, pausing for some time before she murmured, "Yes."

His brows tightened. Her fingers had slowed their massage, but she hadn't drifted to sleep.

"Jessie?"

She didn't answer.

He pulled her chin up, looking deep into the light blue eyes. The sparkle he'd seen a few minutes ago had faded.

"Jessie, what's wrong?"

"Nothing, nothing's wrong." She lied, he'd bet his bottom dollar.

"Aren't you happy?" he asked, his heart jolting

at the thought.

A smiled formed. "Yes, Kid, I'm very happy."

"Well then, what's wrong? Don't lie to me, I can tell you're sad."

"No, really, I'm not sad. It's just..."

Soft skin flowed beneath his thumb as it circled her mouth.

"It's just what?" he asked.

"Well, sometimes I feel so happy it-it scares me. I know it sounds dumb, but I've never been truly happy before, and it scares me. It's like I know something has to happen to take it away from me."

"Jessie, my sweet Jessie." He leaned forward, letting lips replace the movement of his thumb.

"Don't be frightened. Nothing's going to happen. I promise." He resettled his hand then lifted her body to rest atop his. Warm and inviting, soft mounds and luscious curves pressed against his flesh.

"I plan on spending the rest of my life making you happy," he whispered, wanting her again.

She kissed him back, long and passionately, ready and willing to fulfill his every need. Her eagerness turned the blood in his veins to rivers of hot lava. The covers slipped away as their zeal grew, taking over every thought other than desire for one another.

Hours later, while Jessie slumbered at his side, Kid's wandering mind kept him awake. Something was going to happen, he just didn't know what is was or when it would happen, but he sensed it.

Montgomery still hadn't surfaced, and the cattle rustling Hinkle had mentioned had happened at the ranch. The herd of young stock, grazing a couple miles from the house had been hit- hard. Almost a hundred head missing, and Skeeter and Russell hadn't returned yet.

Skeeter had sent a wire, saying something came

up and it would be a few more weeks before they returned. The muscles in his neck grew stiff. He'd sent the two on a ghost hunt, nothing he needed or wanted. It hadn't been safe for Russell to remain at the ranch, or any where near. Not because of Montgomery, but because of himself. If Joe hadn't pulled him off Johnson the evening he returned from Dodge, he would have killed the man.

The arm around his wife tightened. He still might. It was probably a good thing something came up, keeping the two away for a while longer.

Jessie stirred and he realized it was his strong hold disturbing her sleep. He relaxed his arm as she mumbled and twisted in her sleep. He waited for her to resettle before following the movements of her body to spoon his long frame to hers. His fingers flayed over her stomach and pulled her bottom against his groin, her back to align with his chest. Burying his face in the long tresses, he closed his eyes, and waited for much needed sleep to overtake his mind.

The faint howl of a lone brush-wolf filtered in through the open window. Kid's tired, weary mind caught the sound as if it was meant for him. Was his destiny to become as lonely as the wolf sounded? Jessie had a forgiving soul, but would she forgive him for murder? No matter how much he tried to deny it, it was sure to happen. He was bound to kill her brother.

Chapter Thirteen

Sammy rose from the ground near her feet. Ears perked, eyes peered on the driveway leading into the yard, he let out a sharp bark. Jessie let the shirt fall into the wash bucket and turned to the barn as Kid stepped out of the wide door. He kept his eyes on the road while walking across the yard.

Her husband arrived at her side as Joe and two other ranch hands positioned themselves beside the barn, bunkhouse, and corral gate. Jessie knew why Jed Montgomery looked for her, and accepted the fact he'd show up one day, whether he'd hurt her or kill her brother is what she didn't know.

Kid's comforting arm folded around her as a wagon rounded the corner. "Who is it?" she asked.

"I don't know," he said.

Wind tugged at the arched canvas covering the back of the long wagon bed which two horses, heads hung low, pulled closer to the house. The quick clops of another horse sounded behind her. Jessie twisted as Bug leaped from the horse coming to a stop beside Kid.

"It's an old woman and young girl, Kid. Ain't no one else with 'em," the youngest brother explained.

The corners of Kid's mouth lifted as the hunched form driving the tired horses lifted an arm in greeting.

"Well, I'll be damned," he murmured.

"What? Who is it?" Jessie asked, squinting against the sun. Her eyes popped open, and happiness floated across her chest.

"It's Willamina! Kid, it's Willamina!"

"Yes, my dear, it is." His long strides kept pace with her scurrying feet as they rushed to the wagon.

"I see ya found her," Willamina said to Kid while pulling the team to a stop.

"Yes, thanks to you," Kid said.

The woman laughed. "Glad to be of help."

"Willamina! It's wonderful to see you!" Jessie looked at the Conestoga wagon. "Are you heading west?"

"Good to see you too, girl. You're looking mighty pretty." Wrinkles formed between her thin brows and she nodded at Kid.

"He treatin' you right?" Willamina asked.

Jessie smiled and raised a hand to pat her husband's chest, fingers taking a moment to absorb the steady beat of his heart. His eyes met hers, sparkling with delight.

"Yes, he treats me very well."

Willamina nodded. "Good." She looked toward the girl sitting beside her. "This here is Eva Robertson."

"Hello, Eva," Jessie said.

The girl, no more than fifteen or so, looked up and gave a slight nod of greeting. Cheerless, brown eyes glanced between her and Kid before they fell back to the hands in her lap.

Willamina tugged on one of her earlobes. "Eva's papa was killed a week ago. They were just traveling through, on their way to California." The woman looked at Kid. "I thought I might take you up on that offer. I had to get her out of Dodge, and it's too late in the year to head west."

Kid took a step toward the wagon. His hand rose to help the old woman down.

"I'm glad you did." Lowering Willamina to the ground, he glanced over his shoulder. "Bug, help Eva down and then take care of these horses."

Bug scampered around the back of the wagon, and Jessie stepped forward, hugging her friend close. "It's so good to see you."

"Did that man of yours tell you I could stop by?"

Jessie glanced to her husband. The love she felt for him grew every day.

"No, no, he didn't tell me that. But he did tell me it was a very kind woman who told him I was at the soddy."

Kid's deep, smoldering eyes met hers. His gaze filled her heart with sunshine. "And I'm so very happy he found me."

The wink of his eye made her cheeks burn, not with embarrassment, but promise. She glanced back to Willamina. "And I'm excited he invited you to the ranch."

Kid stepped forward, one hand coming to a rest in the small of her back. "Let's go into the house. I'm sure Willamina and Eva could use a rest."

"Yes, let's." Jessie motioned for Eva, who stood on the other side of the horses, to join them then looped an arm through Willamina's.

"We just finished dinner. It'll only take a minute to warm it up." Eva followed behind, Jessie turned. "Do you like chicken and dumplings, Eva?"

"Yes, Ma'am," the girl, head hung low, answered.

Jessie saw herself, a few years ago, in the girl-sad, distressed, and alone. Kid's hand slipped to her hip to give a reassuring and understanding squeeze. Her head leaned against his shoulder for a moment. She was lucky, so very lucky.

There were times she worried. Fretted he'd tire of her and wish he'd gone ahead with his plan of going to Europe and marrying a refined, well-bred wife. He reassured her over and over again he had no regrets, no desire for any woman but her. Still, she couldn't help the doubts and uncertainties that over took her mind sometimes. A few months of happiness, no matter how wonderful, couldn't wash away years of disappointments.

Kid, pulling her to a stop outside the back door, broke her thoughts. He motioned for Willamina and Eva to step inside and while they did, he lowered his face.

"I love you," he whispered before kissing her.

It wasn't a quick peck, but a slow, sensual meeting of lips. A kiss that made her heart pound and her stomach flip.

When it ended, she said, "I love you too, so very, very much."

****

Kid reached over to squeeze the trembling fingers lying on the table. His wife turned, a forced smile on her lips.

"She looks so sad," Jessie murmured.

"She is. Poor little gal," Willamina said.

After eating a small amount of lunch, Eva insisted on seeing to the care of her horses and walked out the back door.

"What happened?" Kid asked.

Willamina shook her head. "She and her pa were with an earlier train, but separated when her ma became ill. After she died, they moved on, got to Dodge a little over a week ago. They camped near the tents, just for the night.

"Someone slit her dad's throat and would have had his way with her if'n some of the men at the city hadn't heard the ruckus." Her green eyed gaze landed on him. "The killer got away, but, Kid, it was Montgomery."

Jessie gasped. He tightened the hold on her hand and a tremor tickled up his spine. He stiffened his shoulders, trying to hide his fear.

"How do you know?"

Willamina pointed a thumb toward the back door.

"The girl's description. I went to the sheriff, he said Montgomery had been in town, drove in a hundred or so head, claimed they were strays and such he'd found.

Sheriff said they weren't, they were young stock. Well fed, young stock. No one at the yards would buy the cows, thinking they were stolen. He thinks Montgomery took the stock toward Abilene. He went after him and I," she paused, shrugging her shoulders. "Well, I thought it would be safer if Eva and I wintered out this way."

Kid rubbed his jaw, mulling the story.

"Good thinking, Willamina. You and Eva can stay here with us."

"Naw, you newlyweds don't want an old woman and young girl underfoot." She looked at Jessie. "I was hoping if'n no one was using your soddy, maybe Eva and I could winter there."

Jessie leaned over, placing her creamy white hand upon the woman's worn red one. "Willamina, you wouldn't be underfoot. We'd love to have you stay with us."

The woman shook her head. "Naw, we'd rather have our own place. Especially Eva, she has some healing to do."

"Well, if that's what you'd prefer, of course you can use the soddy." Jessie turned to him, asking, "Can't she?"

Kid, the back of his mind focused on the fact the cattle Montgomery had closely matched the ones he was missing, patted her cheek.

"Of course she can. It's your place, Jessie. You can do whatever you want with it." He stood, kissed the top of his wife's head then turned to Willamina.

"The place still needs a lot of work before it's ready for winter. I'll go talk to Joe, have him send some boys over there and by next week you and Eva can move in. Until then, you'll stay here with us."

Willamina nodded and stood. "I'll walk out with ya. See if I can convince Eva to come into the house for a bit." She turned to Jessie. "I'll be back to help you with the dishes in a minute."

"No, I can clean this up myself. You go see to Eva, she needs you." Jessie rose and expectantly raised her face to him.

Kid smiled, forever happy to do as she asked, kissed her soundly, and then led Willamina to the door.

Walking down the steps beside him, Willamina said, "They're your cows, aren't they?"

"Sounds like they could be."

"You see Montgomery around?"

"Nope, but I've been a bit preoccupied."

She laughed- a light, young, carefree laugh. "She's bit you good."

"Yes, she has." He didn't mind admitting it at all.

"She's quite smitten herself."

Kid smiled and knowing he'd found a confidant in the old woman said, "If she loves me half as much as I love her, it'll be enough to last a lifetime."

"Have you told her that?"

"What?"

"That you love her!"

He chuckled. "Yes, I've told her."

"Good. Be sure you do it every day. A woman can't hear it enough."

"I'll remember your advice." Kid kept his steps short, walking beside her across the lawn.

"That no good brother around?"

"No, not right now. I sent him north with one of my brothers. Told them there was some land up that way I was interested in. They're supposed to scout it out, look for ground water, and whatever else. I just wanted him out of here for a while, until I can figure out what to do with him."

Willamina chuckled. "Besides kill him?"

Kid guffawed, the old woman knew him well. "Yeah, besides kill him."

"Good luck with that one." Willamina patted his arm then turned to where Eva sat on the back of the covered wagon, head bowed.

Kid glanced between the girl and the old woman. "Good luck to you, too."

She nodded.

"Let us know what we can do to help," he said, and meant every word.

Willamina stopped, turning back around to face him.

"Hey, Kid?"

"Yes?"

"You think that brother of hers got anything to do with those cows of yours? The ones Montgomery's got? Maybe he done hit your brother in the head and paired up with Montgomery."

Kid blinked. The thought hadn't crossed his mind. But now that Willamina said it, it seemed to take root. His blood turned cold. She still looked at him, clearly waiting for an answer.

"I hope not, Willamina. For his sake, I hope not."

****

After her guests were settled down for the night, Jessie let Sammy outside one last time. Anxiously tapping a toe, she waited for the dog to finish his business and return to the door. Kid had gone upstairs a few minutes ago. Her body trembled, thinking of joining him. Antsy, she opened the door.

"Come on Sammy, get in here."

The dog, tail between his legs, meandered in, looking at her with droopy, brown eyes.

"I'm sorry, but it's late." She patted his head and pointed to the rug near the fireplace. "Go lay down, now. I'll see you in the morning."

Without waiting to see if he obeyed. She blew out the lamp and ran to the stairs.

Breathless from the speedy flight, she leaned against their bedroom door as it closed behind her.

Kid lowered a book, sending a startled look her way.

"What's wrong?" he said, flipping the covers aside to rise.

She held out a hand to stop his movements. "Nothing." She gathered the bottom of her nightgown and lifted it over her head. It floated to the floor as she walked toward him.

"I was just afraid you'd fall asleep before I got up here."

Sitting on the edge of the bed, he reached forward. His long fingers folded around her waist, the touch was heaven to her naked flesh.

"You could have always awakened me." Kid pulled her closer.

She stepped between his knees and placed her hands on his shoulders.

"I hadn't thought of that."

He leaned forward, the heat of his mouth moved over her shoulders, then lower.

"Remember it. Always."

She ran her fingers through his thick, sleek hair, tipping her head back in pleasure.

"I shall. Always."

A yelp, followed by a giggle, left her lips as he unexpectedly lifted her up and flipped her around. She landed on the mattress and Kid straddled her, planting his knees next to her hips. His face lowered.

"You better."

"Always," she sighed. Her hands came up to cradle his handsome face.

"I love you," he said.

Freshly shaven skin glided beneath her fingers. "I love you."

His hands slid up and down her sides, the slight touch full of delight and making her skin tingle. One hand paused then slipped beneath her back. Something hard moved below her and she arched, giving him room to pull it out. Kid held up the book he'd been reading. Jessie laughed and reached for it.

"What were you reading?"

He tossed the book on the floor. "I couldn't even tell you." His lips went to her throat. Feather light kisses sent flutters of pleasure across her neck.

"Have you read all of the books in your library?" she asked.

Between nips, he answered, "Yes, some twice."

Her fingertip traced a circle on a wide shoulder blade.

"Have you read all of the newspapers and magazines too?"

Propped on his elbows, he lifted his head.

"Most of them. When did you become so interested in my reading?" He kissed the tip of her nose.

"Just curious, that's all."

"A few minutes ago, you were worried I'd be asleep." His lips touched hers. "Remember?"

"Yes, I remember." She ran her tongue over his lips.

"Mmm. I bet you're curious to know if I ever read the *Waverly Library* tablets as well."

Her body stilled, and her mouth gaped before she closed it, pinching the tip of her tongue between her teeth. She flinched at the pain, and then bit down on her bottom lip.

Kid chuckled, his eyes laughing as they gazed down at her.

"You left them in your bedroom when you left for

Boston."

"When you sent me away to Boston."

"Where you never arrived." He kissed her again. "Thank God."

"So did you read them?" she asked.

"Yes, I read them." He repositioned, bracing his body with one hand while the other ran across her cheek. "I figured I could use the education when I finally found my wife."

A twinge shot across her chest, the pain quick and sharp like a bee sting.

"What's that look for? You didn't like the stories?" he asked.

Jessie tried to soften the grimace on her face and shrugged.

"There's an awful lot of kissing in them."

He leaned down and nuzzled the sensitive spot behind her ear.

"You don't like kissing?"

She turned her head nestling her nose under his chin.

"I like being kissed by you."

"Good. I like kissing you. Now, come here." His fingers spread through her hair to pull her head to his. "Enough about books, I want to show you a few other things I like doing with you."

Jessie joined his lovemaking wholeheartedly, even though in the back of her mind a little thought tried to remind her she wasn't the reason he'd read the stories. She wasn't the wife he'd always wanted.

****

The November air had a nip to it, but Jessie didn't mind, joy kept her warm, even during the ride from the sod house to the ranch. Rosebud, the timid mare Kid had given her, was gentle and easy to control. And with her husband, riding Jack next to her, not even a winter blizzard could chill her.

"Thank you," she said, giving Kid a sideways

glance.

"For what?"

"For fixing the soddy up so nice for Willamina and Eva."

He reached over, took her hand, and held it as the horses walked along the road.

"I didn't do that. Joe and the boys did."

"Yes, but you told them to. You paid for it, right down to the new, wood floor."

"You're welcome. But, Jessie, don't you know I'd do anything for you? I'll forever do anything I can to see a smile on this beautiful, little face."

Her face grew warm and tingly.

"You make me blush," she admitted.

"Hmm," he said. "When we get home let's see how else I can make you blush."

She giggled. "Well, then let's hurry." With a slight kick from her heels, Rosebud leaped forward, changing their slow pace to a quick, fast gallop.

Still laughing and motivated to get the evening meal over quickly, Jessie leaped down as soon as the horses stopped near the barn. But Kid wasn't smiling. Confused, she followed his gaze to where it had settled on two horses.

"What is it?"

Kid didn't answer. Instead, he flipped around to look at the bunkhouse.

Her heart hit the ground. A cold chill sent all the warmth from her body. Russell and Skeeter stood on the porch. They stepped down and began walking across the dirt.

One hand became warm, and wondering how, she looked down to see Kid's large fingers wrapped around hers.

"Hey, Kid. Hey, Jessie," Skeeter said.

"Skeeter," Kid greeted.

"Hi, Jessie," Russell said.

"Hello," she choked. Life as she knew it was

over. Done. Over. The thought made her shiver. Kid tugged her hand. Gratefully, she stepped closer, but even the invisible, protective shield she felt in his arms couldn't stop her brother and his schemes.

"We just got back a couple hours ago." Skeeter smiled from ear to ear, like they should be happy to see him.

Jessie bit her lip. There was no reason for her not to be happy to see Skeeter. He'd been very kind to her.

"W-we're glad you're back," she said.

"I'll meet you in the bunkhouse in few minutes," Kid said, turning her toward the house.

"Uh, Jessie, can I talk to you for a minute?" Russell asked.

A hammer began pounding in her temples. Kid looked down at her. She opened her mouth, but didn't know what to say, so closed it, and shrugged her shoulders.

"What for?" Kid asked.

"Well, uh, well, I just want to apologize." Russell kicked at the dirt, his eyes down cast. He did sound sincere, but then again, he'd sounded sincere before.

She looked at Kid. His expression said it was her decision. Russell was her brother and she owed him a chance to change, didn't she? Still unsure, she nodded.

"All right, come into the house. You too, Skeeter," Kid said.

Instantly, Skeeter was walking beside her. "Hey, Jessie, you got any of those molasses cookies?"

"Yes, in the kitchen," she said.

Skeeter glanced at Kid, "Mind if I go get a couple?"

"Go ahead," Kid said.

"Hey, Russ, come on, these are the ones I told you about," Skeeter said.

Russell looked at Kid as well.

"Go on," Kid said.

Skeeter and Russell walked around to the back of the house while Kid led her to the front steps. After he let Sammy out, he helped her remove her coat.

Jessie checked her hair in the mirror, retying the bow holding the long mass away from her face, and generally wasting time.

Behind her, Kid appeared in the mirror. "You don't have to talk to him."

"Yes I do. He's my brother."

"And Skeeter's mine," he said, a glimpse of humor in his dark eyes. His head came forward, nuzzling the back of her neck. "I love you."

She twirled into strong arms, absorbing his love, strength, and optimism. "Stay with me?"

"Forever," he whispered before covering her mouth with his.

"Hey, you two coming in here?" Skeeter's muffled yell sounded from the kitchen.

"Hold your horses, Skeeter, we're coming," Kid answered.

Jessie giggled, half in humor, half in nervousness. Kid took her hand and they walked into the kitchen. He pulled her chair out, eased her into it, and then sat down beside her. Heavy, thick silence filled the air.

Russell thudded his fingertips against the table. "Well, like I said. I just want to apologize, Jessie. I said some pretty mean things to you. I didn't mean them." He scratched his head. "I don't know what else to say. I know I've done some pretty stupid things. And I really don't know why I did them. It was just that sometimes...I'd...well I'd get scared knowing I had to take care of you. I didn't know how to take care of myself, let alone someone else. And over the years, it just kind of got worse and worse. I just want you to know I'm sorry for the way I treated you. I really am."

Across the table, the look on Russell's face wasn't his classic, 'I'm sorry' one. It looked real, sincere. Jessie blinked, wondering what clouded her vision. A hand ran over her back, smooth and comforting and another pressed a white handkerchief into her palm. She used it to wipe at the tears on her cheeks before she said, "I forgive you, Russell."

"I promise to be a better brother from now on, Jessie." He blinked then pressed a heel of one hand to the corner of his eye.

Weary, and more than a little confused, she nodded. "Thank you." Had six weeks on the prairie with Skeeter changed him?

The room remained silent for several minutes before Skeeter said, "So, Kid..." He swallowed the cookies in his mouth before he continued, "We found that land you were talking about. It's not good for much, not even grazing. Hardly a drop of water anywhere around."

"Oh," Kid said, his hand still running over her back.

"But, we found another chunk. If'n you really want to buy some, that's the chunk to buy."

"Oh, yeah? Why?"

Skeeter, eyes wide, lips grinning, nodded as he said, "Because there's dinosaur bones on it. Lots and lots of dinosaur bones."

Chapter Fourteen

"Dinosaur bones?" Kid thought he'd heard it all. Leave it to Skeeter to astonish him.

"Yeah!" Skeeter dug into his pocket then laid five black triangular shaped things on the table. "And sharks teeth."

Kid rubbed his forehead. "Sharks teeth?"

"Yup."

"What would I do with sharks teeth and dinosaur bones?" he asked.

Skeeter played with the little, black teeth. "People back east, they'll pay big bucks for them. Won't they Russ?"

Russell nodded. "They're called paleontologists. We ran into one out by the chalk pyramids. We rode with him to the Castle Rock Badlands. He said folks out east are starving for this stuff."

Kid pushed the silliness of their finds to the back of his mind and brought up another subject.

"Did you run into any one else during your excursion?"

Russell and Skeeter looked at each other.

Skeeter answered, "No, no not really. A few prospectors here and there. A family or two traveling west."

"No one by the name of Montgomery?"

Russell's head snapped around. His gaze dashed between him and Jessie.

"Jed Montgomery?"

"Yes, Jed Montgomery," Kid said, ire ripping up and down his spine.

Russell looked at Jessie. "Did he hurt you?"

She shook her head.

His Adam's apple bobbed. "Was he looking for me?"

"I don't know. I haven't seen him. I asked if you two did," Kid said.

"Nope, name doesn't ring a bell to me," Skeeter said, chomping on another cookie.

"So, he hasn't been here?" Russell asked.

"No," Kid said.

Russell turned to Jessie. "He's that mean one from Dodge."

"I know who he is," she said.

"Well, you stay clear of him, ya hear?" Russell said.

Skeeter glanced around the table, brows furrowed. He scratched his chin. "So, Kid, what ya think? Ya interested in this land?"

"No, Skeeter, I'm not interested in any land with dinosaur bones and sharks teeth," Kid said.

"Damn," Skeeter sighed. "I think I'm going to head home then, see what ma and the boys have been up to."

Russell stood. "I'll head back to the bunk house. Whatever Joe's cooking for supper sure smelled good."

The two collected their hats and meandered out the door. Kid turned to Jessie.

"How are you doing?"

"I'm fine," she said. "He almost sounded sincere."

"Yes, he did." And Kid didn't know what to do about it. Then again six weeks with Skeeter could probably make anyone question their own sanity.

She scooted her chair away from the table.

"Where are you going?" Kid asked.

"No where. Just going to cook us some supper."

"Oh," he said, twisting his chair out from under the table, ready to watch her float around the kitchen. On second thought he grasped one of her hands.

"With all the talk of dinosaur bones and sharks teeth I guess I forgot the time."

Jessie smiled. One of her lovely, just for him, smiles that made her eyes sparkle and his groin throb. She hoisted her skirt and flung one leg around to sit on his knees as if they were Rosebud. Her hands went around his neck.

"Well, I hope you haven't forgotten what else you had planned for the night."

He flicked his eyebrows, enjoying her game. "Oh, you mean the part about making you blush?"

"Ah," she said. "You do remember."

"Tell me, sweet Jessie would you like to blush in the kitchen?" He started to unbutton the front of her dress.

"But it's supper time," she said, not trying to stop him at all.

"I don't mind if we eat late," he pressed his nose into the hollow of her throat.

"I don't mind either," she whispered.

****

A lone steer cut itself from the herd, heading toward the row of trees near the bottom of the gulley. Kid waved an arm at Russell, signaling he'd go after the cow. Giving Jack his head, they angled across the hill to cut the steer's path before he reached the bottom. Jessie's brother had been back over a week and had behaved himself the whole time. Actually, Kid was beginning to like him. He had a good head, when he used it right, and he was no longer afraid of a day's work.

Lost in thought, Kid missed the quick turn the

cow took and almost lost his balance as Jack cut left going after the steer. Settled back in the saddle, he took a second look toward the trees. Something had moved. Perhaps a deer, he put his attention back on the steer. Jack ran below it. With legs bounding in all directions, the cow twisted and headed back up the hill.

He reined Jack in and waited for a moment, making sure the steer headed toward the rest of the herd before he swung the horse around. Whatever was in the trees deserved another look, might be a cow he hadn't realized was missing.

Clumps of trees, stripped of their leaves, ran along the small creek and provided cover for critters of all breeds. Jack plodded along while Kid searched for the red-brown of a steer. A snap, loud enough to make Jack jump, sounded and Kid pulled on the reins, trying to calm the horse. The next crack echoed and sent Jack into a rear. At that moment, Kid realized the sounds were something ricocheting off the horse's flank.

Legs stiff in the stirrups, he absorbed every jolt as Jack ended his rear with several four-legged hops. Getting the horse under control, Kid whipped Jack around and spurred him to the trees. Through the barren branches, he saw a man on a black horse race across the creek.

Kid ducked his head and twisting his neck every now and again to miss the larger branches from knocking him off Jack, he took chase. Further down the gully, the trees thickened, forcing him to slow and pick a trail through the brush. By the time he arrived at the creek, the man and horse were little more than a dot on the horizon.

Wiping at a sting on his cheek, he glanced down. Blood smeared across the back of his hand. Several branches had smacked his face, more than one hard enough to scratch his cheek. Rubbing at the pain in his shoulder, where another limb had bounced off, he dismounted and walked to the creek to rinse his hands and face.

The cold water stilled his breath for a moment and sent a shiver down his back. Shaking off the feeling, he bent to retrieve his hat. A few feet away, a tiny river of black ran toward the water. His gaze followed the flow backwards into the brush. He stood, and walked over to flip a few tall bushes out of the way.

His hands froze.

"Shit!"

He bent down and rolled the man onto his back. The body was warm, pliable. Kid hoped he was still alive. Optimism dissolved when he noticed the long, jagged cut below the man's chin. A thin, waning trickle of blood slowly oozed from the long slit across his throat.

He scanned the area, a few feet upstream a small campsite had been built. A hole had been dug in the ground for a fire pit and the ground had been well trampled. Warmth crept along his cheek again, and he ran the back of his hand over the still bleeding scratch. He rubbed his hand across his thigh and wiped the scratch again before pulling the bandana from around his neck and pressing it to his cheek.

A thrashing noise sounded up the hill. He took a couple steps up the embankment then heard Russell's voice.

"Kid? Kid?"

"Down here!" he yelled.

Russell and his horse burst through the trees.

"You all right? We got worried when the steer came back but you didn't."

"Yeah, I'm fine. But there's someone else that's not," Kid answered.

Russell dismounted and picking his way down

the hill with the side of his boots, he made his way through the second clump of trees.

"What happened?"

"I don't know. I saw something while chasing the steer and came back for a look. I noticed a man on a horse and took after him, but by the time I got through the trees he was gone. Then I found him." He pointed to the dead man a few feet behind them. "Better go tell Joe to send one of the boys for Turley."

Russell moved closer to the body. He stumbled and held one shaky hand out.

"Kid, we don't need the sheriff. Only you and I know about this. We can bury him right here and no one will ever know anything."

Kid frowned. "What? Of course we need the sheriff. This man was murdered."

Russell looked around, scanning the area. "You say there was someone else?"

"Yes, there was someone else. A man on a black horse. He ran off that way." Kid pointed over his shoulder, stepping closer.

"Why are you bleeding?" Russell waved a hand at Kid's shirt.

A long smear of blood ran across his shirt and the front of his pants. "Damn that scratch must have bled more than I thought." He wiped his fingers over his cheek. They came back clear. "A branch caught me on the way through the trees."

Russell took a step backwards.

"Honest, Kid, I won't tell anyone. Hell, I wanted to kill the bastard myself."

The hairs on the back of his neck stood to attention.

"Who?"

Russell pointed at the dead body. "Montgomery."

Another loud crash sounded before Kid had a chance to say anything.

Joe's voice echoed down the hill, "Kid? Kid, you down there?"

"Yeah, Joe, we're down here," he answered.

"What's up?" Joe asked from the other side of the trees.

"Got a dead man, Joe. Send one of the boys to Nixon," Kid said.

"Kid," Russell said, shaking his head. "They'll hang ya for this Kid. Sure as shit, they'll hang ya."

"They aren't going to hang me, Russell. I didn't kill him."

Russell, as white as a sheet, looked at him. "I hope they believe you. For Jessie's sake, I hope they believe you."

A chill, colder than ice, vibrated Kid's spine.

****

Jessie paced the floor. Something had to be wrong. Kid was never this late. For the umpteenth time, she opened the back door and peered into the dark night. Ted, one of two ranch hands who'd stayed at the house today, sat on the top rung of the corral. From his high seat he could see both entrances of the house and the long driveway. She nodded at his wave and closed the door.

She had no reason to be afraid, Sammy sat near the stove. The hands guarded the property, but all the same she was frightened. For lack of anything better to do, she stirred the pot of beans again and banked the fire in the stove. Closing the fire door, Jessie knelt down and wrapped her arms around Sammy.

"He's always home before sunset, Sammy. Always."

A roll of thunder sounded. She pulled her head up and listened closer.

"It's horses. He's home!"

Jessie lifted her skirts and rushed to the front door, throwing it wide open as she ran across the porch and down the steps. Two horses separated from the half dozen trotting toward the barn. Her hands flew to her chest as she noticed an empty saddle on one. Turning to the two coming to a stop in front of her, she glanced between Russell and Joe.

Her mind must be playing tricks on her. She looked again, first at Russell, then Joe. Both of their faces looked, sad, sullen. She glanced back to the rider-less horse. Her heart stopped. It was Jack. Jessie's feet began to move backwards. Her head shaking with disbelief, a sob burned her throat as it exited.

"No, no!"

"Jessie, it's not what you think." Russell dismounted. "Kid's all right."

She locked her knees to keep them from buckling.

"Then where is he?" Her eyes narrowed as he walked closer. "What have you done?" She turned from her brother and asked, "Where is he, Joe? Where's Kid?"

Russell touched her arm. "Jessie-"

She pulled away from his grasp. "Where's my husband?"

Joe took her other arm. "Come in the house Jessie, we'll tell you what happened."

"What happened?" She looked at Russell. "You said he was all right!"

Joe wrapped his other arm around her shoulders. "He is all right. He's just been arrested."

"Arrested? For what?"

"For killing Jed Montgomery," Russell said.

"Oh God, no." Her knees buckled.

Joe caught her before she slid all the way to the ground. She leaned against him and even accepted Russell's help as the two men ushered her into the house.

****

Before first light she rode out. Not one of the men would allow her to go to town to see Kid, but then again, not one of the men had snuck in and out of places like she had. Nobody at the ranch would even miss her until well after breakfast. By then she'd be in Nixon.

She hadn't made it mile up the road when Russell caught up with her. Without slowing Rosebud's steady run, she looked over her shoulder.

"There's no one else. Just me, figured you might need some help," Russell said above the roar in her ears.

She didn't answer. A piece of her was thankful. She'd never broken someone out of jail before and might need Russell's help. Of course, breaking Kid out wasn't her first choice. Her first choice was to convince Turley there was no way the tender, kind, and loving man she married could ever kill anyone.

Rosebud's sides heaved. Jessie slowed her pace, not wanting to wind the horse.

Russell drew his horse beside her.

"You know, Nixon doesn't even have a jail."

"It doesn't?"

"Nope. But they got an old well they put the prisoners in."

"A well?"

"Yup, Turley got the idea from Dodge. Before they built the jail there that's what they did. Just lowered them down in the ground and hoisted them up when their time was done."

"So Kid's in a hole in the ground?" she asked.

"Afraid so, Jessie."

She spurred Rosebud back into a run. Nixon wasn't that far, surely the horse would be fine.

The little pony was tired, but not winded when they rode into Nixon. Russell pointed to a grove of trees near the outskirts of town. An old well, complete with a high rock wall surrounding it, sat a few yards in front of a cluster of barren trees. The empty branches made Jessie realize how cold the morning air truly was. She jumped from Rosebud and ran to the rocks.

Leaning over the side of the wall, she yelled, "Kid?"

"Jessie?" echoed up from the bottom. His deep voice sent a new pain across her chest.

"Jessie, what are you doing here? Be a good girl and go home. I'll be along shortly."

"Not hardly," the sheriff's gruff voice responded.

Jessie flipped around. "Sheriff Turley, I demand you let my husband out of this well this minute."

"Oh, you demand it?" the man guffawed.

"Yes. You had no right to put him down there."

The sheriff laughed harder then squinted beady eyes. "It's called murder, darlin'."

"He didn't murder anyone," she insisted.

"Oh, were you there?"

"No, but I know my husband. He couldn't murder anyone."

"Yeah, well I've known your husband a lot longer than you have, and I believe he could."

Jessie stomped her foot. "Oh, you're a spiteful man."

Turley smiled, "And you're quite a spitfire."

"Jessie? Jessie!" Kid called from the well.

She rushed back to the edge, and leaned over, unable to see anything but a dark hole.

"Yes?"

"Jessie, who's with you?" Kid asked.

"Russell rode to town with me, he's right here." She waved her hand behind her, telling Russell to step closer.

"Russell." Kid's voice sounded low and slow, like when he talked to one of the brothers after they'd made him mad.

"Yeah, Kid?" Russell asked.

"Take your sister home and keep her there."

"We already tried that, Kid." Joe's voice sounded on her other side.

Jessie turned to stare with disbelief. Had the whole ranch followed her? Maybe she wasn't as good at sneaking around as she thought.

"Hey, Joe," Kid said. "Glad to hear your voice."

"You doin' all right down there?" Joe asked.

"I'll be doing better when I know Jessie's back at the ranch," Kid replied.

Something in her snapped. Not in pain, but in anger and it fueled determination. They all thought she was nothing more than a pretty wall flower, someone who should sit back at the ranch, prim and proper, being protected by all the men folk. Well if that was the wife Kid Quinter wanted, he'd better go to Europe and find one.

Jessie glared down the dark hole, faintly making out the silhouette of man. And when he did find one, she'd scratch the woman's eyes out and put her right back on the ship she sailed in on.

She flipped around and growled, "Just what is your plan, Sheriff? That is if you do have one."

Turley frowned, scratched his whiskered chin and said, "Yes, I have a plan. The circuit Judge will be in town next week. He'll hear the case and decide whether Kid swings or not."

She swallowed past the thick lump in her throat.

"You can't keep him in that hole for a week. It could snow any day."

Turley shrugged. "He's got a blanket."

Jessie clutched her hands into fists, wishing she could box his big nose. "And what about the other man that rode away from the scene?"

"Well, Ma'am, I for one don't believe there was another man."

"You incompetent little weasel! Of course there

was another man," she screeched so hard her vocal cords hurt.

"No one saw anyone else."

"Kid did!" Tears burned the backs of her eyes.

Joe laid a hand on her shoulder. "Come on, Jessie, Kid's right, let me take you home."

With a side step and a rough tug, she slipped out from his touch. "I'll go home, when I'm good and ready."

"Jessie! Listen to Joe, sweetheart. I'll be home in a few days." Kid's voice echoed up the side of the well.

Whether it was the well, her frazzled mind, or Kid, but for some reason, his voice didn't sound right, not nearly as strong and righteous as usual. Was it fear? Did he believe he may swing from the tree branch? Did he believe there was no one to save him?

Jessie looked down the dark hole again, this time clearly seeing the handsome face of her husband. Her heart somersaulted, and fortitude settled in her mind.

"All right, Kid. I'll go home. And I'll see you in a few days."

He smiled. A wide smile just for her. "I love you."

"I love you, too."

The smile left his face. "Good-bye, Jessie."

"No, I won't say good-bye. It's not a good bye." She swallowed the sob in her throat. "I'll see you in a few days."

He nodded. She turned and without a word to any of the men standing around, pushed her way past them to mount Rosebud. She'd go home when she was damned good and ready. But if telling Kid she would, helped ease his mind, then so be it. He'd saved her life, now it was her turn to save his.

After flipping into the saddle, she turned the

mare down the road. Russell's horse fell into step beside her. "Joe's staying to talk with Turley."

She nodded.

"Where are we going?"

"Stephanie Quinter's," she answered.

Russell nodded and they both nudged their horses into a faster canter.

****

Fine puffs of dust trickled from the walls surrounding him. Kid stepped to the center of the hole as a few larger chumps of earth broke loose. The departing hooves from the horses above vibrated the ground, knocking the air-dried soil from the steep shaft. Wafting little clouds of earth away from his face with one hand, he sighed. Thank goodness Jessie had listened to him. She'd be safe back at the ranch, now he just had to figure out a way to get out of this hell hole.

Maybe he should have listened to Russell; Turley wouldn't listen to the truth, instantly the man had concluded he'd murdered Montgomery. Kid twisted the tension from his neck. Jessie, his sweet Jessie would be left alone if he hanged. Oh, she'd have his family, they'd see she was taken care of...Ah hell, what was he thinking? His family couldn't take care of themselves, let alone his wife.

Wife...How lucky he'd been in finding her. A smile touched his lips. The one thing his family had done very well- found the perfect wife for him. Thank God he'd found her at the soddy before Montgomery.

He tipped his head up. "Joe? Joe, you still up there?"

"Yeah, Kid?"

"Ride out to the soddy, ask Willamina and Eva to come into town. They can identify Montgomery as the man who attacked Eva's father."

"How's that gonna help get you out of the hole?"

Joe asked.

"I don't know yet. I have to think," Kid admitted. "Did you send a wire to Hinkle?"

"Yeah, woke the agent up last night, while Turley was puttin' you down there," Joe answered.

There...there...there....echoed against the sides of the dirt walls. The fading sounds emphasized his location. Kid kicked at the dirt beneath his boots.

"Turley still up there?"

"No, he headed toward his house. Said something about gettin' you something to eat."

Higher in the sky, the sun's rays bounced a little lower on the walls above his head and lifted the darkness around him a small amount. The hole seemed smaller, the walls closing in on him as the area lit up. Kid shook his shoulders in offense to the quiver running up his spine.

"Kid? Kid you all right?" Joe asked from above.

No! No! I'm not all right! Kid wanted to shout. Instead he said, "Yeah, Joe, I'm fine. Go ahead and head out. Stop at the soddy then go to the ranch. Make sure Jessie's all right."

Joe leaned over the edge. "Sure thing, I'll be back later."

"No, no, until Hinkle arrives, there's nothing you can do. Stay at the ranch." Kid ran a hand over the soil in front of him. Cold dirt crumbled beneath his touch and fell to the floor.

"Stay at the ranch and keep Jessie safe. She'll be afraid, Joe. She doesn't like being alone."

Or was it him that didn't like being alone? It had been the longest night of his life, sitting in the deep pit, longing for his bed, his wife's soft body snuggled close to him. Her breath, warm on his chest, sighing in slumber was the sweetest lullaby.

He heard Joe's departing voice, but didn't respond, his mind reliving nights of love making instead. He leaned against the dirt, crossed his arms, and closed his eyes. After finding her at the soddy that morning, he'd sprinted her home, as fast as Jack could carry them. Once at the ranch, before she had a chance to protest, or an opportunity to question his actions, he swept her into his bedroom to fully and completely make her his wife.

A smile pulled at the corners of his lips. She hadn't objected in the least, a matter of fact, she'd surprised him with her eagerness and with fervor led him to unbelievable heights- just as she'd done every night since.

Kid balled his hands into fists and snapped his eyes open. *He'd find a way out of this damned hole*! No one was going to take away the life he'd dreamed of having. The life he'd found with Jessie.

Chapter Fifteen

Stephanie Quinter walked out the front door as Jessie pulled Rosebud to a halt.

Breathing hard, Jessie sucked in air before saying, "I need the boys."

"What's up?" Stephanie asked, stepping off the porch.

Fighting the pain in her chest, Jessie said, "Kid's been arrested."

Stephanie's eyes grew wide. "Shit! Who'd he kill?"

"He didn't kill anyone!" She said. Why was she the only one who knew that fact?

"Then what's he been arrested for?"

Russell stepped down from his horse. "Murder," he said.

"Shit!" Stephanie exclaimed.

"That he didn't commit!" Jessie glared at her brother.

Russell nodded- a nervous little up and down head shake. "Right."

Stephanie twisted her head, shouting behind her, "You boys get out here, now!"

Bug, the first out the door, popped the remains of a biscuit in his mouth.

"Hey, Jessie! What you doing here this morning?"

"Your brother's done killed someone," Stephanie

said.

Ready to snap, Jessie screeched, "No, he hasn't!"

Skeeter stepped forward, around Hog and Snake.

"Who?"

Jessie leaped off her horse, hitting the ground with a force that made her ankles burn.

"Damn it! Kid didn't kill anyone!" She ignored the pain and stomped forward.

The four boys and Stephanie took a step backwards.

She thrust a finger at them. "Do you understand that?"

They nodded.

"Then I don't want to hear it." Her eyes burned as she stared at each one. "Ever again!"

They nodded again. Skeeter sidestepped, scooting behind Hog. She stopped his slither with a solid stare. "Skeeter, go saddle a horse, you have to go find a marshal."

"Huh? Me? What for?"

"Because Turley is trying to frame Kid, we need a marshal to override his authority."

"Override Turley?"

She glared at him. "Yes, a sheriff is elected by the town folks, but a marshal is appointed by the government." She straightened her shoulders, almost surprised by everything she'd learned reading Kid's books. And from Kid, books were nothing compared to the things he'd taught her...

"Really?"

She wasn't sure who asked the question and had to blink several times before her mind cleared. Her brows tugged at the skin between her eyes, she rubbed the area.

"Yes, really. Ride south to Sequoyah County, there's a new marshal's office there."

"All right, Jessie." Skeeter jumped from the

porch to sprint to the barn.

"Hog and Snake, you saddle up too," she said.

"Sure, Jessie. You want us to ride with him?" Hog asked.

"No, there's a man on a black horse you and Snake are going to find. He's the real killer, so take a gun."

They glanced at one another before looking back to her. She almost chuckled. They were kind, gentle boys, and a tug in her chest made her recognize how much they'd come to mean to her. But it was time for them to grow up, become men.

"Russell knows what direction he took off, he'll ride with you."

"Ah, Jessie-" her brother started.

She glared at him. It was time for him to grow up too. "What?" she seethed.

His body stiffened. "Nothing."

Bug stepped down from the porch and came to stand beside her. "What about me, Jessie? What can I do to help?"

She looked into young, sad eyes. Of all the boys, he looked the most like Kid. Her heart tumbled, and she swallowed the lump in her throat.

"I need you to take clean clothes and food into Kid. Turley has him down in an old well. It's bound to be cold down there." Jessie had to stop talking. The lump had come back, it was too large to maneuver around.

"All right. I'll go saddle up too."

She nodded. A light caress ran over her shoulder. Jessie glanced from the hand to the woman who owned it. A wide smile covered Stephanie Quinter's face.

"I knew I'd made the right choice, giving you to Kid."

The tears behind her eyes tried to jump forward, but Jessie straightened her shoulders, pulling strength and determination from her core. She couldn't break down now- she was a cattle baron's wife, and it was her job to protect her husband's assets, including his life. The potency of her fortitude kept the tears at bay.

"Yes, Stephanie, you made the right choice, and I thank you for it."

Stephanie wrapped her arms around Jessie. "It's 'Ma' to you."

A warm rush raced through her veins and at that moment Jessie realized she didn't just have a husband, she had a family. One she loved very, very much.

Stephanie stepped back, tilting her head toward the barn.

"The boys are ready. What I can do?"

Jessie tipped her head toward the porch, the spot Stephanie had rushed to when she and Russell had galloped into the yard.

"Loan me your gun," she said.

With the double barrel shot gun tucked between her hips and the front swells of the saddle, she led the boys out of the yard and down the road to the ranch. She kept the pace fast, not allowing anyone the chance to speak. When they came to the first Y in the road, she nodded to Skeeter.

He touched his hat and steered his horse down the southern path. The rest of them rode on, making a short trip of the long ride. Sammy met them before they rounded the calving pens. Without missing a step he swung around to run beside Rosebud back into the ranch yard.

Jessie had already sent Hog, Snake, and Russell after the murderer, and was loading Bug's horse with a bundle of food, including several molasses cookies and a warm coat for Kid, when Joe rode up. He dismounted and walked toward her. She patted Bug's leg. "You remember everything I told you to tell Kid?"

"Yes, Jessie. You're here at the ranch. The boys are all home with Ma," he said.

"Good. Go on now."

The horse twisted and Bug used the reins to slap it across the rump. Dirt rose and small pebbles flew against her skirt as the horse took off. She turned to Joe and flipped her head toward the barn where several ranch hands meandered about.

"What are they doing?"

Joe squinted at the men with a confused looked. "I don't know. I didn't tell them to do anything when I left. Just took after you and Russell."

"Well, I suggest you tell them to get busy. We have a ranch full of cattle that need to be rounded up before winter sets in. Until Kid gets home we're a man short, therefore we don't have time to lollygag."

Joe looked at her. His eyebrows rose.

She lifted hers.

A smile touched his lips. "You're right, Mrs. Quinter. I'll get 'em movin'."

Jessie nodded a stiff, proud, rancher's wife nod and then turned to stroll into the house. Kid was right, she always had a choice. She could sit around and do nothing, whining, crying, and missing her husband with all her heart. Or she could find the real killer, keep the ranch running smoothly, and miss her husband with all her heart.

By the third day, her determination was waning. The sun, turning the eastern sky a soft pink, would soon announce another morning without Kid at her side. Arms folded, she hugged herself, pressing her chin to her chest.

Hog, Snake, and Russell had returned last night, having found no sign of a man or a black horse. She'd interrogated them, making sure they'd performed a thorough search and finally had to oblige they had. No campfires, no broken grass;

nothing but empty gullies and barren plains for miles.

Jessie lifted her head and after one last glance at the morning sky, moved across the room. The snap of the bedroom door closing behind her, echoed down the hall. She leaned her head back and lifted a hand to her chin. Of course the man wasn't anywhere near where he'd killed Montgomery. They'd been watching the cattle, their rustling interrupted by the men rounding up the young stock.

She pushed away from the door and marched down the hall, rapping on the doors to the rooms she'd put the boys in the night before.

"Get up!"

Groggy eyes and tousled hair popped out from behind each door.

"Let's go," she said, moving to the wide staircase.

"What? What is it?" Russell asked.

"I know where to find that man." She scurried down the steps, whistling for Sammy as her feet stepped off the last one.

****

Kid lifted a leg over the rock wall of the well. The other one followed, a deep sigh left his chest when both feet settled onto the top soil. Relief at being out of the hell hole quickly turned to anger. He flipped around, hand stretched out, ready to grab Turley by the neck.

Turley took a step back and before Kid could move forward a solid grasp landed on his forearm.

"Whoa, up there, Quinter," George Hinkle said.

Kid shook off the hold.

"I've been in that damn hole for three days, while this idiot sat around doing nothing to catch the real killer."

"Yeah, well, you're out now and Dickson and I are going after Buckley," Hinkle said.

"Buckley?"

"Yes, he was Montgomery's partner," another man said.

Kid looked at the man. A round Marshal's badge, pinned to his chest, sparkled in the afternoon sunlight.

"Who are you?"

"Marshal Clyde Dickson," the man said, holding out his hand.

Kid shook it.

"You're the new Marshal stationed in Sequoyah County?"

"Yes," Dickson said.

A loud huff sounded. All three men looked toward Turley, his expression clearly displayed he was the only one who didn't know about the appointment of a new marshal. Kid turned back to the other men.

"You know this Buckley?"

"Yup, another gunslinger. He and Montgomery worked for Hughes. He'd hired them to keep the rustlers from getting his cattle. Turns out, they were the rustlers. And that black horse you seen Buckley on is a prize stallion he stole from a rancher up by Abilene. The man's fit to be tied," Hinkle explained as he held out Kid's gun belt.

"Have you been tracking Buckley too, Marshal?" Kid took it and wrapped the leather around his waist.

"No, I haven't had a chance to go through all the warrants at my office yet. I had just arrived at my post when your brother showed up," Dickson said.

Kid's hands stopped, the leather lace wrapped around his knee went lax in his fingers.

"My brother?" He scanned the area. Near a trio of horses, Skeeter raised a hand in greeting.

"Yes, your wife told him I could override Turley's arrest, and let me tell you, I had no choice in riding over to investigate the charges." The Marshal let out a slight laugh. Not an irritated groan, but a friendly chuckle.

"Oh," Kid murmured as he finished tying the holster to his leg. Then the first part of the man's sentence resonated.

"My wife?"

"Yes, and she was right. I do have the authority to override the local sheriff. And did, especially after everything Hinkle told me." The Marshal waved at Hinkle.

Jessie, his sweet Jessie, full of wonderful, soft, warm kisses, and hot, passionate love, had known what to do. While he sat in the hole, racking his brain, she'd found the answer and acted. He'd thank her for it as soon as he arrived at the ranch- he'd thank her for saving his life.

"Thank God you arrived when you did, Dickson. I've been arguing with this blockhead since sun up. I would have ended up shooting him if you hadn't walked in when you did." Hinkle pointed to Turley.

George's voice pulled Kid back to the present. He slapped the man on the shoulder.

"You still can."

"You want me to arrest you again?" Turley slapped his hand on his gun, ready to draw.

Kid rolled his eyes. "Ah, hell, Turley I was just kidding." He turned, facing the local sheriff eye to eye. "When are you going to get over it?"

Turley squinted, pulling his eyes into tiny slits.

Hinkle stepped closer. "Get over what? What's going on here?"

Kid let out a deep sigh. "Once, over ten years ago, I danced with his wife, Emma Sue at an Independence Day celebration. She wasn't his wife then, but it doesn't really matter. I wasn't interested in her, never have been, never will be. But for some reason, for years he's thought I'm head over heels in love with her and goes out of his way to make my life miserable because of it."

"That true, Turley?" George asked.

Turley stiffened, his chin jutted forward. "Emma Sue tells it differently."

"What does she say?" Marshal Dickson asked.

"She say's he hounded her. Begging her to marry him," Turley said.

Pointing a finger at Kid, he continued, "How about all those times you've stopped by to see her?"

Kid frowned. "What times?"

"Every time I'm out of town?"

"I've never stopped in to see her. Not once." Kid shook his head.

"What about last week?" Turley challenged.

"Last week? You know I haven't been to Nixon in well over a month," Kid answered. He almost felt sorry for the man. Emma Sue was clearly playing him.

Turley looked down, the toe of his boot scuffed at the dirt. "I know."

"Malcolm," he said, stepping closer to the man. "I swear to you, I have never stopped in to see your wife, not when you were home, and not when you were out of town. You know me. Until I met Jessie, I didn't give a woman, any woman, a second glance." He smiled. "Hell, I still don't, Jessie's all I'll ever want, all I'll ever need." His chest tightened.

Turley nodded.

Not caring if the whole world knew how he felt, Kid continued, "I love my wife and she loves me. I'd never do anything to jeopardize that."

With pride he squared his shoulders, happy to give credit where credit was due. "And it's because of you that I have her," he held his hand out. "Thank you."

Surprised, Turley looked up, then back down at the proffered hand.

Kid moved the hand forward, encouraging the man to take it. Malcolm did and as they shook hands, Kid said, "A wise old woman told me you can't tell a woman often enough that you love her. Maybe that's what Emma Sue wants to hear."

Turley furrowed his brows, then a slow smile formed and he nodded. "Maybe you're right." He shook Kid's hand harder and added, "That wise old woman wouldn't happen to be the same one that dropped the rope down the well the other night?"

Kid laughed, remembering how Willamina had tried to break him out the second night he was in the hole.

Turley chuckled and gave him a slap on the back. "You're welcome. I'm really glad things worked out for you and Jessie."

A thunder of hoof beats made Kid turn from the Sheriff. Bug pulled on the reins, bringing the horse to a skidding halt.

"Kid! Kid! They let you out!"

Kid ruffled Bug's windblown hair before his little brother had a chance to retrieve the hat that flew off his head as he jumped down from the horse.

"Yes, they let me out. You can leave the food Jessie sent in your bag." Bug had come to see him everyday, his saddle bags full of food and clothes from Jessie, including her wonderful molasses cookies. He couldn't wait to get home to see her.

He turned to Hinkle and Dickson. "I have to get to the ranch."

Hinkle said, "We'll ride with you, see if we can pick up Buckley's trail."

"Fine, I'll even introduce you to my wife. You can see for yourself she's the prettiest thing on earth." He slapped Hinkle's back. "And she's mine, all mine," Kid said before he turned to walk toward his other brother.

"Skeeter, let me take your horse, you can ride

with Bug. I'm anxious to see my beautiful wife."

"Ah, Kid?" Bug said. "Jessie ain't at the ranch."

An icy quiver shook his spine, stopping his steps. "What? Where is she?"

"I don't know." Bug shrugged, shaking his head.

"What do you mean, you don't know?" Kid balled his hands. "Who is at the ranch?"

"Just Ted. The rest of the hands are out roundin' up cows. He helped me look for her. We didn't find hide nor hair of her anywhere. Sammy was tied to the front porch," Bug said with a quivering voice.

Kid soared into the saddle and without looking back to see who was on the pounding horses behind him, raced the wind toward the ranch.

****

Jessie crouched behind a cluster of sandstone boulders. Two men sat near a small campfire at the bottom of a narrow ravine. For centuries, tributaries of the Arkansas River had trickled through this area of the ranch, cutting out valleys on the great flat land, before drying up or turning course to split through another region of the prairie. The rolling ground made it hard to spot the boys. She hoped they were almost in position, having sent them around the top of the ridge to surround the two men below.

Her thoughts had been right. The man with the black horse was stalking Kid's cattle- her cattle. The nonchalant questions she'd asked Joe hadn't surprised him, not since each morning she'd enquired where the men would be rounding up cattle that day. Today Joe and the ranch hands were finishing up with the herd on the south side, which made her believe the rustlers would be working on the north end, picking on the cows furthest away from the cowboys.

The small group of cows grazing near the men proved her intuition had been correct. Their horses were saddled, and from the looks of the camp, they'd been there a while, but now, having branded the last of the cattle as she watched from the top of the hill, they were about ready to head out.

She looked again, hoping to see signals which said the boys were in place. No one had said what the signal would be, Snake just told her to stay behind the rock, said she'd know when they were in place. All three of them were quite mad at her, deep down she knew it was only because they didn't want her to get hurt. And she wouldn't. She had too much to live for, a lifetime of being Mrs. Kid Quinter.

A sharp crack split the air. She peeked over the rock. The men below drew their guns while running toward a small clump of bushes. Another shot went off and dirt near their running feet puffed in the air. One of the men fired back, up the hill on her right. More shots came, so many she couldn't tell if they were coming from the top of the hill or the bottom. Spooked cattle ran in all directions.

The men below dove into the bushes, all the while faint puffs of smoke billowing from the barrels of their guns. Then came a lull, the air grew quiet. She held her breath, hoping beyond hope that none of the boys had been injured.

The shots started again, she sighed realizing the boys must have needed to reload.

One of the men started to slip out of the bush. His location hidden from the others, she was most likely the only one to see him. Hefting Ma Quinter's double barrel shotgun from the ground beside her, she groaned. The gun weighed more than a full bucket of water. Praying she'd put the shells in the right direction, she laid the barrel across the rock, held the stock tight to her shoulder and squeezing her lids tight, pulled the trigger.

Noise rocked the air and pain ripped across her chest while her head hit the ground so hard tiny white dots formed before her eyes. Coughing at the smell of gun powder, she tried to pull her body into a sitting position, but the pain in her shoulder made her gasp for air, which increased her coughs. Had she been shot? Would she die before ever seeing Kid again? Her eyes stung, whether from the thoughts or from the powder, she didn't know.

More gun shots filled the air. Even with the ringing in her ears, she knew these shots were close, almost flying over her head. She twisted, trying to pull her body from the ground, but froze midway. A large, bulky man, one she'd never seen before, leaped forward.

Big hands grabbed her and pulled, tucking her tightly behind the cluster of rocks.

"Stay down! Keep your head down, little lady."

His thick arm, pressing her against the sandstone gave her no other option and the gun fire filling the air made talking impossible. Within minutes, the popping of rifles ceased, and the man lessened his hold long enough to slip a hand to her elbow, which he used to help her rise.

Below them men scrambled about. Relief made her shoulders relax when she recognized Russell, Snake, and Hog amongst several others. She raised one hand, rubbing at the pain above her right breast.

"Are you all right?" the big man asked. "From the look of that gun of yours, I bet it kicks harder than a mule." He chuckled, a low deep laugh. "But you got him. Filled his backside full of buckshot," he said as he looked down the hill.

Two men, hands and feet tied, hung over a couple of horses; their stomachs filled the saddles as their heads and feet dangled over their mounts. Jessie glanced back to the man.

"Who are you?" Her voice echoed inside her ears.

The man reached out and took her right hand.

She flinched as the movement made her shoulder sting again.

"Oops, sorry," he said and slowly pressed her arm against her abdomen. "There, hold it right there, the pain will ease in a few minutes. My name is Sam Wharton. I own a ranch up near Abilene."

Sam Wharton! The man who'd sent to Europe for a wife.

"W-what are you doing here?"

****

Kid rode into the ranch yard full of horses. Half a dozen strange men mingled about, stopping to stare at his screeching halt. With rocks still bouncing from beneath the horse's feet, he leaped to the ground, then paused, unsure which direction to run.

The back door opened. A ruffled pink skirt dashed out the opening and down the stairs.

"Kid!"

He ran, his feet barely touching the ground. Seconds later his arms caught her as she flew into his chest. Air gushed from his lungs. Kid didn't care; he need didn't air when he had her.

"Jessie, my sweet Jessie."

Her lips, ready and willing, parted below his. With devotion, he consumed them, each and every tiny bit. Moments later, when his mind began to clear, he realized something prevented her body from molding to his. He lifted his head, wanting to rid the interference.

A large, white bandage wrapped around her torso, held one of her arms tight to her bosom.

Startled and concerned he asked, "Jessie, what happened?"

"Oh, I-"

"You need to buy your wife a smaller gun. The one she has pert near killed her."

Kid looked over Jessie's head, to where the

stranger's voice had come from.

"Who are you?"

A tall, burly man held out a hand. "I'm Sam Wharton. You probably don't remember me, but when you were little, you and your pa stopped by my place once."

Wide-eyed with surprise, Kid said, "Yes, I remember."

Sam Wharton glanced over Kid's shoulder.

"Hinkle, the feller you've been after and one of his cohorts is tied up in the barn."

"Buckley?" Kid asked, his hold on Jessie growing tighter.

"Yes, your wife filled his arse with buckshot." Wharton's loud hooting laugh filled the air before he continued, "But that gun of hers bruised up her little shoulder a might in the process."

Kid framed her face, searching the pale blue eyes. Happiness and a hint of guilt flashed at him.

"What gun?" he asked.

"Your mother's," she said, casting her eyes downward. Seconds later, they popped back up and her spine stiffened.

"I had to find the real killer." Tiny fingers ran across his chin. "I can't live without you."

"Nor I without you," Kid admitted, and regardless of the yard full of men, kissed her again.

Someone cleared their throat, forcing Kid to once again halt his obsession for a short time. His eyes met Sam Wharton's.

"What are you doing here?"

"Buckley tried to sell me a herd of young stock. Upon closer inspection, I recognized your brand under the one he'd stamped on them. I've seen your brand quite often, bought a lot of stock you sold to the yards. So, I locked him up in my ice house and sent a man to get the sheriff.

"The rat escaped and stole my prize stallion

before the sheriff arrived. Since I had to hunt him down to get my horse back, I told the boys we'd drive your cattle home at the same time. They're down in the gully with the others your wife stopped those gunslingers from stealing."

Kid looked down at Jessie. A full smile brightened her face and she nodded. His heart jolted. She was so much more than he ever imagined.

"We heard shots and rode in just as your wife shot Buckley. My boys fired some rounds, giving your brothers and brother-in-law time to scale the hill and captured him and his partner. He's been squalling since they loaded him on his horse.

"He admitted to killing Montgomery, and to sling-shooting rocks at you, hoping you'd find the body and get blamed for the murder. Give him free rein to rustle the rest of your cows. At first your brothers had to make him talk then we couldn't shut the sorry arse up." Wharton let out a small chuckle.

Kid looked around, his gaze landing on all four of his brothers, and Russell, a few feet away. Each stood tall and straight. All of a sudden he saw them in a different light. The group was clearly men not afraid of much, and men he'd welcome on his side anytime. He smiled and nodded to his family.

Wharton reached forward, slapping Kid on the shoulder.

"This is a fine spread you've got, twice the land as I've got. But then again you must have twice the brain as I've got. You were smart enough to find a good, solid country gal to be your wife. The prettiest one I've ever seen." He shook his head. "I sent off to Europe for one. It was a disaster. After listening to her cry herself to sleep every night for two years, I shipped her back."

Jessie gasped, her eyes flashing between the kind rancher and Kid.

Sam Wharton patted her good shoulder. "I'd give

everything I own to have the shotgun wielding bride you got." He laughed again. "Quinter, I'd say you are a very smart man."

Kid looked down at her, the light in his eyes made her heart somersault. Jessie welcomed the flip, knowing as long as she lived her heart would forever leap at his nearness. He was her reason for living, the reason her heart beat. His finger, warm and smooth, ran over her cheek bone, sending tingles of delight over the skin it caressed.

"I'd say I'm lucky, Mr. Wharton. I'd say I'm the luckiest man on earth," Kid said, his eyes meeting hers with honesty.

Kissing him with a smile that ran from ear to ear was hard, but she found a way. After all when the luckiest girl on earth was married to the luckiest man on earth, they were bound to be smiling. Always.

A word about the author...

As a young girl I remember spending warm summer days and long winter nights with Nancy Drew and Laura Ingalls-Wilder. As the years slipped by the books evolved into romance novels by Kathleen Woodiwiss, LaVyrle Spencer and a host of others. In 2000 when my husband said I should write one, I took the challenge, and have loved every moment of the journey. To create characters from once upon a time and lead them through a life that ends in happily ever after is such fun. Of course, you have to torture them a little bit along the way, and just like real-life children you often have to clean up after them. But, just like real children, they are worth it. My husband of more than twenty-five years, and I live in Minnesota, have three grown sons and the most precious gift ever-a granddaughter, Isabelle. I work as the resource development manager for our local United Way program, am a life-long Elvis fan (yes, I've been to Graceland) and love spending Sunday afternoons watching NASCAR with family and friends. My previous published works include magazine articles, children's activities and a contemporary romance novel, "A Message of Love" with PublishAmerica in 2005.

Contact Lauri at Lauri@izoom.net

Thank you for purchasing
this Wild Rose Press publication.
For other wonderful stories of romance,
please visit our on-line bookstore at
www.thewildrosepress.com.

For questions or more information,
contact us at info@thewildrosepress.com.

The Wild Rose Press
www.TheWildRosePress.com